Melusine of Lusignan

and the
Cult of the Faery Woman

Gareth Knight

SKYLIGHT
PRESS

© Gareth Knight 2010, 2013

Published in Great Britain in 2013 by Skylight Press,
210 Brooklyn Road, Cheltenham, Glos GL51 8EA

First published in the USA in 2010 by RJ Stewart Books, Lincoln, Illinois.

Designed and typeset by Rebsie Fairholm
Publisher: Daniel Staniforth

Front cover image: from *Les Très Riches Heures du Duc de Berry*, Folio 3.
Back cover: Tour de la fée Mélusine at Vouvant, France. Tradition attributes the
building of the 13th century castle to Melusine. Photo by Alf van Beem.

Photo on p.7 (top) by PHGCOM and (below) by Havang. Photo on p.8 by Havang.

www.skylightpress.co.uk

Printed and bound in Great Britain by Lightning Source, Milton Keynes.
Typeset in Prospero Pro, a font by Tim Rolands.
Titles set in Brilliance, a modern blackletter by Catharsis Fonts, and Leitmotiv
by Bartek Nowak.

British Library Cataloguing in Publication Data:
A catalogue record for this book is available from the British Library.

ISBN 978-1-908011-28-2

Contents

Chapter One

❧

𝕸elusine in 𝕷usignan

ABOUT twenty-five kilometres south west of Poitiers the train that runs across Poitou to the port of La Rochelle passes over a viaduct that spans a great bow bend in the River Vonne. Here, looking out on the left hand side, high as you are, you can see an ancient church that stands on a great escarpment of rock, slightly higher than the train. This is the church of Notre Dame in the little town of Lusignan.

Both church and town are celebrated for having been built by the faery Melusine, along with a mighty castle here, which for centuries was the stronghold of powerful and turbulent lords, a thorn in the side of French and English kings alike, to say nothing of their neighbours. The castle is no more; regarded as a hot bed of sorcery and a bastion of Protestant and English insurgency, it was demolished by Catholic forces after the religious wars in 1575. It was thought too dangerous to be allowed to stand, despite the reservations of Catherine de Medici, who recognised it as a château of supreme beauty as well as strength. An idealised picture of it can be seen in the famous miniature in *Les Très riches heures du Duc de Berry*, complete with figure of Melusine in dragon form flying round the towers.

The legend of Lusignan tells how after a boar hunt, a young knight called Raimondin accidentally killed his uncle, the Count of Poitiers. That same night the despairing young man met the beautiful faery Melusine at a fountain in the forest. She promised to resolve his problems and bring him great wealth and success if he agreed to marry her – on condition that she remain unseen on any Saturday. The pact was agreed and with the help of her magic powers the faery founded Lusignan.

She also gave birth to ten sons, eight of whom were strangely disfigured in some way, although most of them became great lords and even kings. One day, however, Raimondin, driven by suspicions stirred up by his brother, spied on his wife upon the forbidden day. He saw her lying naked in her bath, her usual beautiful self, but from the waist down with a serpent's tail!

All might have been well had he not later publicly accused her of being a demon, whereupon the betrayed faery leaped from a window, sprouted wings and claws, and flew away. Raymondin never saw her again, although she returned from time to time as a traditional *bean sidhe,* when her cries might be heard prior to the death of any lord of Lusignan, or whenever the castle was about to change hands.

A visit to Lusignan in search of traces of Melusine can be something of a mixed experience. At the time of my own visit the railway station seemed to see few travellers and was not even manned. The Font-de-Cé, the fountain where Raimondin first met Melusine, is paved over, and while picture postcards show what it looked like a century ago, it was plainly much like a communal pump, utilitarian rather than magical.

The old town lies at the end of a quiet country road that leads up from the station. At its centre is the church of Notre Dame, on the north side of which is a breathtaking view of the valley of the Vonne and the woods that once formed part of the great and ancient forest of Coulombiers.

The church itself, dominated by a two storey bell tower, has the atmosphere one might expect from a building that dates from 1024 and witnessed much turbulent history, apart from being the focus of a legend. Toward the east end steps lead down into a crypt that lies beneath the sacristy. Here, along with a number of knights of the house of Lusignan, lie incumbents of an ancient priory that was once attached.

Who knows how much of the atmosphere is due to the influence of Melusine (who is discreetly represented with bat

wings and serpent tail at the top of one of the columns) and how much to more orthodox associations? There are certainly strong claims for the latter, for the church has seen the presence of a Saint and King – Louis XI – and of a Pope – Clement V – whilst its foundations are sanctified by the bones of ancient saints.

The north door, that once joined the church to the priory, has an evocative semicircular arch. Its keystone shows a human head with a long beard and the pointed ears of a faun, whilst twenty two other stones of the arch show figures of animals and men. Of the human figures, two are dressed in long robes, one carrying a book before his chest and the other a wand or baton, whilst another is apparently naked and hopping on one leg, and a fourth squatting figure has clawed feet and appears to have its arms tied.

The rest of the figures provide a medieval bestiary, including a goose, a unicorn, a dragon, a leopard, an elephant and a large fish, and the supporting pillars are topped with fighting animals and bundles of vegetable produce. Some think it all represents the Work of Creation along with the virtues and vices of man.

In 1168 the church was much damaged when King Henry II of England, having married Eleanor, Duchess of Aquitaine, captured Lusignan by way of calling his wife's rebellious lords to order, who did not much care for paying taxes to support his northern wars. Then in 1375, in the Hundred Years War, when English archers fired down on the French troops from the clock tower, much of the tower was destroyed by cannon fire. Finally, during the religious wars, cannon destroyed the priory. During the French Revolution the much repaired church became a warehouse but was restored to religious worship in 1802.

As for Melusine, the principal reminder of her in the centre of the town is "Le Café Hotel et Restaurant de la Fée", the ground floor of which, at the time of my visit, was given over to a bar, complete with jukebox and pin tables, where an inquisitive host seemed as curious to see a couple of English visitors as had the guard of the train that left us at the station. Perhaps we had called at the wrong time of year. The only other indication of the faery in the town was a painted tin sign, erected by an aesthetically challenged resident, depicting a naked nymphette with serpent tail and bat-like wings.

A more sophisticated representation of Melusine, a modern sculpture in winged and busty mode, graces the tourist office at the end of the town. Within this building, along with a souvenir shop, is a comprehensive display of the story of Melusine.

Beyond lie the grounds of the castle, which in the 18th century were made over into one of de Blossac's formal parks. In this small park, the formal avenues of trees seem in their regularity resonant with the columns of an ancient castle, and some may feel an ambience that might stem from the watching eye of the faery Melusine. A memorable impression, felt it would seem, by the American scholar Matthew W. Morris who has devoted more than thirty years of his time to critical editions and translations of the Melusine romances.

Referring to the miniature in *Les Très riches heures du Duc de Berry*, which first sparked his interest, he writes in the foreword of his bilingual edition of Jean d'Arras's *Mélusine* or *L'Histoire de Lusignan*:

> "Since my work on the *Mélusine* first began, and over the years that
> I've spent delving into the many successive layers of the Melusine
> legend, I have gradually realized that the image of Melusine
> hovering above the Château of Lusignan is a perfect metaphor for
> the true literary and historical significance of the fairy of Poitou:
> the château itself is the actual concretion of practical power; the
> image of the winged dragon, Melusine, hovering above represents
> the enchantment which invests the real and practical force of the
> stronghold with superhuman valence, imbuing the material form
> with spiritual power that renders the walls of the fortress far less
> assailable, or even approachable, by mere mortals. This was in fact
> how the château was perceived by the inhabitants of Poitou at the
> beginning of the fifteenth century when the miniature was painted.
> This same aura of mystical power would remain suspended above
> the Château of Lusignan until its destruction two hundred years
> later – indeed, lingering on at the site of its ruins even up to the
> present day – outlasting the material form of the castle itself."

His last sentence suggests a similar experience to my own, for I
too have succumbed to the lasting influence of Melusine after
wandering in the park of her castle grounds.

I would, moreover, regard the presence of Melusine as more
than symbolic or metaphorical. There is much to suggest that she
has existed – in part as the guiding spirit of a particular family –
and in part as "a power within the land", an "earth light", of the
Sovereignty of Lusignan, Poitou or even Aquitaine. And if she
was real enough then, she may well be real enough today. An
exploration of which is what this book is all about.

The story of Melusine comes down to us in a comparatively
late version, at the end of the 14th century, although it obviously
contains earlier material. Indeed Jean d'Arras, who was
commissioned to write it, claimed his work to be based upon oral
as well as written sources. We may therefore, despite its late date,
regard it as a "threshold text", containing a hitherto oral tradition.

What we also find as a result of its somewhat late redaction
is the inclusion of a considerable amount of politically motivated
quasi-history. The romance of Melusine was produced by the
book dealer Jean d'Arras to the order of the Duc de Berry in 1393,

and was followed by a version in verse, in 1401, by Couldrette, chaplain of the l'Archeveque family, lords of nearby Parthenay. Couldrette closely followed Jean d'Arras in his story line, but slanted it more toward the interest of his own patrons.

All this occurred in the middle of the Hundred Years War between the Kings of France and England, who since 1337 had disputed ownership of what is now southwestern France. It came at a point critical to both families. The Duc de Berry was on the French side, whilst the l'Archeveque family were on the English – although they did later decide to turn coat. Each family aimed to establish its own claim to the Lusignan heritage, which had become the property of the French crown when the main branch of the Lusignan family died out in 1315, even though it was currently occupied by English forces. Each family decided that literary means might help their cause, evoking local legend and folklore to establish their link to faery origins.

So when we read the romance of Melusine we need to dissect later political material from mythopoeic origins. The basic story of Melusine and Raimondin is the heart of the matter – the well spring from which all else flows – the principle of a faery choosing to take on human form and make intimate contact with a human being.

Quasi-historical elements are grafted into the romance in the form of stories of Melusine's sons. These serve to claim links of the faery family with important dynasties such as Luxembourg, Bohemia, Cyprus and Armenia, but in part are loosely based on certain 12th century historical characters badly misremembered. However it is worth our while to look at the real historical record to see if Melusine may perhaps have acted at times as an ancestral tutelary spirit as well as a traditional *bean sidhe.*

Other mythopoeic fragments are in accounts of one of the sons, Geoffrey Great-Tooth, who achieved the reputation of giant killer, in the course of which he entered a magic mountain to discover secrets of his faery ancestry. Nonetheless he too has links to an historical character who became embroiled in disputes between the Lusignans and another family with claims to faery origins, the House of Anjou, the so-called "Devil's Brood." Of this last, Eleanor of Aquitaine brooks large. Patron of the cult of Courtly Love, she embodied in her own life certain parallels with the faery Melusine.

There are other elements of ancient lore in the faery kin of Melusine. Her younger sisters, Melior and Palastine, guardians of a hawk and of their father's treasure respectively. Her mother Pressine, allegedly a sister of Morgan le Fay, who also married a human, King Helias of Albany. Whilst there is also the mysterious first wife of Raimondin's father, Hervé de Leon, who seems to have acted much like a faery.

From all of this it may be seen that the romance of Melusine of Lusignan is of considerable complexity. Yet, perhaps most importantly, it grips our emotions as a very moving human story. For it could also have profound implications on the relationship between the human and the faery worlds.

In short, does Raimondin, in his betrayal of his faery benefactor, represent a wider failure of the human race in coming to terms with the Otherworld?

That is for us to judge, and if we think it to be true, to try to do something about it!

Chapter Two

❧

The Romance of Melusine

HIS is the story of Raimondin, the founder of the family of Lusignan, and of his lady, who as well as being the daughter of Helias, King of Albany, was of the faery parentage upon her mother's side, Pressine of Avalon.

Raimondin was a younger son of Hervé de Leon from Brittany, who also had his connections with the faery folk. A favoured companion of the King of Brittany in view of his wisdom, courage and skill, as the result of a stratagem set up by false friends at court, he killed the nephew of the king. As a result he was forced into exile, leaving all he had in the hands of his enemies.

He journeyed south and east through the high mountains that contain the source of the Rhône, until he met, by a fountain, a beautiful lady of great wisdom and power. They married, and she advised and supported him well. Although the rough country had not yet been inhabited, they built castles and founded towns and caused the land to prosper, so that in a short time many people lived there. Seeking a name for the country they called it Forez on account of the forests with which it was covered, and so the region is named to this day.

However, there came a time when a quarrel developed between the knight and his lady. The reason for this is not revealed, only that she left him suddenly. Desolated though he was by her desertion, of which he never spoke the cause, honour and prosperity continued to come his way. The barons of the realm sought a new wife for him, one of high birth – and chose the sister of the Count of Poitiers. Together they had several sons, the third of whom, Raimondin, was well gifted, handsome and full of grace.

When Raimondin was fourteen or fifteen years of age, his uncle, the Count of Poitiers, organised a great feast for his son Bertrand who was about to be made a knight. He invited many local barons, including his kinsman the Count of Forez, along with his sons.

There were jousts with many fine prizes and the rejoicing went on for a week and a day. When it was over the Count of Poitiers invited Hervé of Forez to leave Raimondin behind. He promised that his nephew would have a fine future and he would treat him as if he were his own son.

Count Aymeri was a man of great repute, not only for his nobility and generosity but because he was most learned in astrology. Some said the greatest known since Aristotle. Raimondin in his turn was devoted to his uncle and did all that he could to please him.

The count loved hunting, and had many hunting dogs and birds of prey of all kinds. One day a forester came to say that in the forest was an exceptionally large and fierce wild boar. The count, delighted at the prospect of unusual sport, summoned his men and his hounds on the morrow, with many knights and lords and Raimondin, as ever, close beside him.

When they came to the forest the hunt began. The boar was fierce and fearless and charged with such ferocity that no hound dare confront it. Nor would any huntsman approach it with his spear. Or any knight or squire dare put foot to ground.

When the count arrived he poured scorn on all of them. "What?" he cried, "Is a son of a sow going to frighten you?"

At this, Raimondin was so ashamed that he leaped from his horse, spear in hand, ran straight at the boar and struck it between the shoulders.

The boar dodged and threw him to his knees, and before the young man could stand up it turned and shot off with such speed that no hound, knight or huntsman could follow it. However, the count and his nephew pursued it fiercely, out-distancing the others, so excited were they by the chase. They had good horses and followed the trail of the boar when it was lost to sight.

Eventually night fell, and they stopped under a great tree. Here they dismounted and decided to wait until moon-rise.

While Raimondin lit a fire, the count, knowledgeable as he was in astrology, looked up at the stars shining brightly in the clear sky. After gazing at them for some time he sighed deeply, and then began to pray.

Soon after, the moon rose, full and clear and Raimondin called to the count to come to the fire and warm himself. But the count was more concerned with what he had seen when gazing at the sky, where he foresaw awful and amazing things. Among which, as he told Raimondin, that if at this hour, a subject should kill his lord, he would become rich and powerful and honoured, and bring forth a noble line that would be remembered until the end of time.

Raimondin could not bring himself to believe that such a thing could be true: that a man should obtain good fortune and honour from having committed mortal treason.

Yet as they spoke they heard within the wood the sound of breaking bushes and branches. Raimondin took up his spear, the count drew his sword, and they waited beside the fire. With a crash the monstrous boar reappeared, frothing at the mouth, showing its teeth, and about to charge.

Raimondin leaped toward the beast, spear in hand, but the boar turned and ran at the count, who seized a spear, wedged the shaft under his foot, and pointed it toward the boar to impale it on the point. But the boar charged with such force that it brought the count to his knees.

Raimondin ran in, brandishing his spear to strike the boar that the count had overturned. But as the beast righted itself to charge once more, the blade of the spear glanced off the hard bristles on its back and flew from Raimondin's hand. It struck the count, running him through the chest. Raimondin pulled out the spear and pierced the boar with it, which fell stone dead. Then he turned to the count and tried to revive him, but in vain. His uncle was dead.

At the sight of the wound and the blood which spurted from it, Raimondin was overcome. He deplored with heart-rending groans the foul and perverse fortune that had caused him to kill the man he loved best, who had been so kind to him.

In what country could one who had committed such a crime find refuge? Surely he would be condemned to die a shameful death, with great torture, for committing such grave treason. He prayed the Earth might open and swallow him up, and found no consolation in the prediction that if such an adventure arrived it would bring great honour and high lineage. He could see nothing but the opposite. He would be the most despised and unfortunate of men. The best he could hope for was to fly the country and go in search of adventure in some place where he could perhaps expiate his sin.

He embraced his lord for the last time, and weeping, left him lying dead in the forest by the fire, along with the body of the boar. Mounting his horse, he set off through the forest, prey to such terrible sadness that he cared not where his way might lead.

At midnight he passed by a spring which was called the Fountain of Thirst. It was held by some to be enchanted, because in times past great and marvellous adventures were said to have happened there. Some even thought they still did from time to time. The spring sprang up at an impressive site, below a wild escarpment of great rocks, in a beautiful meadow that ran the length of the valley below, up to the verge of the forest.

The moon shone clearly as Raimondin's horse carried him where it willed. Its master simply sat upon its back, deprived of all will, as if he were asleep.

At the fountain three ladies were playing, but Raimondin passed by without seeing them.

The eldest of the maidens knew very well who he was and ran after him. She seized the horse's bridle and pulled it up short.

"Well sir knight," she said, "is it through pride or ignorance that you pass fair ladies without saluting them?"

He did not speak, still without hearing or understanding.

She feigned anger. "What, young dreamer?" she cried, "Do you not deign to speak to me?"

Still he said not a word.

"Well," she said, "Either you are deaf and dumb or else asleep on your horse. But I know how to make you talk, as long as you know how!" So saying, she took his hand to pull him from his steed.

Raimondin started like a man suddenly awakened, and grasped his sword, thinking enemies had seized him.

The lady laughed at him and said: "Sir knight, do you want to fight? You have no enemies here. Good sir, I am on your side!"

Then Raimondin saw her and was dazzled by her beauty. He thought he had never seen any lady so fair. He leaped from his horse and bowed before her, making excuses for his rudeness.

She asked where he was going at this hour, for if he did not know the way she could help him, as there was no forest track or path that was not known to her.

Raimondin thanked her for her kindness but replied evasively that he had lost his way for most of the day.

To this she replied, "Raimondin, why do you try to hide the truth from me? For I know very well what you have done."

On hearing his name, Raimondin was so confused he did not know what to say.

"Why try to deceive me?" she said, "I know very well you have killed your lord by mistake, and would not have dreamed of doing so. I know all that he said to you from his knowledge of the stars."

Raimondin was yet more stupified and admitted the truth, but asked how could she know? How could anyone have told her about it so soon?

She told him not to be surprised at all she knew and declared that she was the one who could help him find honour and profit from out of his adversity.

Although he might think that she and her words were an illusion and work of the devil, she told him she was nonetheless part of God's world, and believed all that a good Christian should. What is more, without her and her counsel he could not survive the adventure. Yet if he did believe in her, then all that his lord had predicted would come to pass – and even more. He would become a great lord and his line a most powerful one in the world.

Hearing these promises Raimondin thought of the words of his lord. He also thought of the dangers in which he ran, to be killed or exiled, hunted through all countries where he might be recognised. He decided therefore to take the risk and believe the lady.

He thanked her and swore there was nothing he would not do in order to please her, however difficult or painful, as long as it was honourable.

She replied that she would advise nothing from which prosperity and honour would not come. That he should not be afraid, for she was of God, but he must agree to marry her.

Raimondin eagerly replied that he would, but then she asked him to promise something else, even if he did not understand it. He must swear, most solemnly, that upon a Saturday he would never seek to see her, or even discover her whereabouts. For her part, she would do nothing that was not to his glory and honour.

So Raimondin swore and the lady began to instruct him.

"Go directly to Poitiers. When you get there people will ask if you have news of your lord, the count. Tell them that you have not seen him from the time your pursuit started. Say that you were lost in the forest and are as surprised at his disappearance as everyone else."

"A little while later foresters will arrive, carrying the count, dead, on a litter. All will assume that the wound was made by the tusks of the boar. They will say that the boar did him to death just as he killed the boar, hailing it a remarkable exploit."

"Go into mourning like the others, and dress in black. There will be a great funeral and a day fixed when the barons take their oath of loyalty to the new young count. Come back to see me on the eve of that day. You will find me here again."

To celebrate their love, she gave him two rings, with stones that had great power. One would protect the wearer from perishing in combat and the other, if the cause was just, would give its wearer victory, whether in court of law or in combat. He might therefore go in safety, and have nothing to fear.

Raimondin took leave of her by taking her in his arms and kissing her. He was now so taken with her that he held for true everything that she said. He went on his way to Poitiers and the lady returned to the fountain with her two companions.

When Raimondin arrived at Poitiers he found several lords returned from the hunt, some the previous evening, others in the morning, who asked him if he had seen their lord.

"What?" he exclaimed, "Has he not returned?"

They assured him that he had not, whereupon he replied that he had not seen him since the time the hunt started, when the hounds started to bay after the boar.

The hunters then began to return in greater numbers, one after the other, but with regard to the count, everyone said the same thing as Raimondin. Some said that they had never seen such an amazing hunt, nor a boar so large or so extremely fast. Others added that it must be a boar that had come from elsewhere and had strayed from its usual haunts. Everyone was surprised that the count had not yet returned.

They gathered around the gate leading to the forest and stayed there waiting for him. Hunters continued to arrive saying like the others that they had spent the night in the woods, unable to find the least path. Meanwhile the countess waited in the great hall along with her children, concerned at the absence of the count.

Then those waiting at the town gate saw a large troop of people returning from the hunt, and heard their lamentations: "Weep, weep, all of you. Dress yourselves in black. That son of a sow has killed our good count Aymeri."

So they entered the city, loudly crying their grief. With them came two foresters carrying, on a horse, the monstrous boar. Then came a litter on which the count lay dead. When the people saw this their despair burst into moaning and wailing as they followed the body to the castle. The funeral was held, with all due ceremony, at the church of Our Lady at Poitiers, after which, mad with anger and grief, and cursing whoever had suggested the hunt, the people took the boar and burned it on a pyre in front of the church.

Finally, the day was fixed for the barons of the realm to give their oath of allegiance to their new young lord and to renew the endowment of their lands. When he heard this, Raimondin mounted his horse, left Poitiers alone, and entered the forest, faithful to the promise he had given to the lady.

He passed the village of Coulombiers and entering into the forest eventually came to the meadow, at the foot of the rocky escarpment which overlooked the fountain. On approaching, he saw a stone building that resembled a chapel. Although he had passed this way many times, he had never noticed it before.

What is more, he was amazed to find a number of ladies, maidens, knights and squires waiting there, who greeted him with joy and respect. They helped him to dismount and led him to meet the lady who awaited him in a sumptuous pavilion. She took Raimondin by the hand and led him in to sit on a splendid couch while the others waited outside.

Then she said to Raimondin: "I know you have acted as I suggested, but now I have to place greater confidence in you. Tomorrow the barons of Poitou swear allegiance to the young count Bertrand. Make sure you are there, and do as I say.

"Go forward and ask a boon of the young count in reward for your service under his father. Tell him you will not ask for anything that will cost him greatly. I know he will grant this boon, for his barons will advise him to do so. When he has promised, ask him, on this rocky escarpment, for as much land as you can enclose in the hide of a stag, and not as a fief, and neither with oath of allegiance nor rent to pay to him or anyone else. This he will grant you willingly. Have it written into a charter, sealed with the great seal of the count, and also those of his peers.

"The next day you will see a man carrying a bag containing a deer hide tanned in alum. Buy it for the price he asks, then cut a single strip as thin as you can from it, in a way that I shall show you. After that, return here so that the boundaries may be traced by it according to my plans.

"Now go bravely, my friend, and fear nothing, for your enterprise will be successful. The day you take possession of the gift, bring the maps and come back to me here."

He promised to do as she said and they embraced tenderly and took leave of one another.

When Raimondin arrived back at Poitiers he found the high barons of the region gathered to swear allegiance to the young count at the church of St. Hilarion.

When this was done, Raimondin stepped forward very solemnly, and said: "Barons of the noble county of Poitou, I pray you hear the request that I make to our lord the count, and if you find it reasonable, pray him of his goodness to grant it to me."

"We will do so willingly, Raimondin," they replied.

Raimondin began to speak very calmly: "Most dear lord, I ask, in respect of the service that I have rendered to my lord your father – God rest his soul – to be so good as to grant me a boon that will cost you little: neither fortress, nor castle, nor anything of value.

"If it pleases my barons," replied the count, "it will please me too."

"If it is something that costs so little," said the barons, "you can hardly refuse."

"Then ask as you please, and I will grant it," said the count.

"My lord," said Raimondin, "I thank you. I ask nothing more than that you grant me, above the Fountain of Thirst, in the rocks in the high woods and in the escarpment, as much ground as it pleases me to take as can be enclosed within the hide of a stag."

"I'faith," said the count, "I can hardly deny you that! I grant you this land in complete freedom: neither to me or any other will you owe either payment or allegiance."

Raimondin knelt, thanked him and asked that a charter be drawn up. This was done in most heavy parchment, sealed with the great seal of the count, and witnessed by the council and peers of the county, who added their own seals, twelve in all, to affirm the legality of the gift.

Then they left the church of St. Hilarion and went to the great hall of the castle where they held a great celebration, with a sumptuous banquet and music. The count distributed rich presents and Raimondin impressed all with his good looks and imposing bearing.

The next day he rose early and went to hear mass at the abbey of Moutier-Neuf. Here he prayed God to permit and bless his enterprise and, the mass over, he left the abbey and saw before the door a man carrying a sack on his shoulders. The man approached him, saying "My lord, will you buy a deer hide I have in my bag? It would make good hunting jackets for your foresters."

Raimondin asked him how much it would cost, and without haggling, took him back to his lodgings and paid him. Then he took the hide to a harness maker and told him to cut from the hide a strip as thin and fine as was possible in the way that he had been shown. He then rolled it up into a great ball of thread and returned it to the sack.

When those delegated to measure out his land arrived with Raimondin at the mount by the meadow, they took out the hide from the sack, and seeing it cut so finely were most surprised, and confessed that they did not know how to proceed. Then two men came up, dressed in homespun robes, and announced that they had been sent to help in the task.

They made a skein of the strip and carried it to the bottom of the valley, as close as possible to the rock. There they fixed a solid stake to which they attached one end of the line. One of them gathered stakes, that he planted all round the rock, from place to place; the other followed, attaching the strip to the stakes. Thus they made a tour of the whole mount until they came back to the starting point.

Here they found that there still remained a great length of leather and this they drew out, proceeding downwards and then along the whole length of the valley. As they did so a stream arose behind them, flowing with a strength that could turn many mills. The count's envoys were astonished not only by the stream beginning to flow but also at the amount of ground that the deer skin enclosed – more than two leagues in circumference. They left for Poitiers and reported to the count and his mother these amazing events.

They agreed that Raimondin must have found some marvellous adventure in the forest of Coulombiers, especially near that spring at the foot of the rocks, where extraordinary sights had often been reported. They wished Raymondin good luck, and prayed that he might makes the best of it.

Raimondin arrived later, bowed before the count and thanked him for his generous gift. The count said he had been told that some very strange things had happened at the place that Raimondin now owned, and prayed to be told the truth of it.

"My lord," replied Raimondin, "I simply liked to frequent this place because it had a reputation of being good for adventures. All that has happened to me there has seemed good and above board. Please ask no more, for I know not what else I can tell you."

The count said no more, for he liked Raimondin well and did not wish to offend him. Raimondin took his leave and returned

to the high forest of Coulombiers, where he descended the mount
and arrived at the spring. Here his lady greeted him with great
joy for his ability in keeping secrets, and said that if he continued
like this, great prosperity would be assured. But before anything
more could be achieved they must marry.

Raimondin said he was ready for that here and now!

"No," she replied, "there is rather more to it than that. You
must go and invite the count, his mother and all his court to come
to our wedding, here, in this meadow, next Monday. Then they
will see the great magnificence I intend to deploy for your greater
glory. They must not think you have married a woman of lesser
condition than yourself. Tell them you are marrying the daughter
of a king, and nothing less.

"However many are invited, they will be well received and
lodged, have no fear. There will be plenty for them to eat and also
for their horses. Go, and do not worry about anything my friend."

They embraced lovingly and Raimondin rode back to Poitiers.

He found the count, his mother and many barons of the region
who bade him welcome, but were stupified when he asked them
to do him the honour of attending his wedding next Monday at
the fountain.

The count remonstrated with his cousin for thinking about
taking a wife without turning to him first for advice. Raimondin
begged him not be angry, saying that fate has such power that
it arranges things as it will. And he was so far engaged in the
arrangement that it was not possible for him to withdraw, even
if he wished.

The count then asked at least to be told the name of the woman,
and her lineage.

"In faith," exclaimed Raimond, "you ask me questions to which
I do not know the answer, for I have not asked them myself."

"This is unbelievable," cried the count. "You are going to marry
and do not know to whom, nor to what family she belongs?"

"My lord," said Raimondin, "if that suits me, then I pray that
it should suit you. If I have not chosen aright it is I who will
have to suffer the pain as God wills it."

"Certainly," replied the count, "you are right. As for me, if there
is a dispute, do not ask me to resolve it. I simply pray that God will
bring you joy and good fortune. We will come to the wedding and
will bring our mother and many other ladies and our barons."

They spoke of it no more but the next morning the count dictated numerous letters to his vassals round about, asking them to accompany him to Raimondin's wedding.

During this time the lady made splendid preparations in the meadow above the spring. All was magnificent and nothing lacked. Such was the splendour one would have thought it was a reception for a king.

On the appointed day everyone prepared to go to the wedding and set out on route together with a fine escort: the count, his mother, his sister and all the barons, and also the new Count of Forez, Raimondin's brother.

When they arrived at the mount above the meadow they saw below them many beautiful rich tents of all sizes and shapes had been erected, and were astonished. They also saw many ladies, maidens, knights and squires; a multitude of running horses – destriers, palfreys and coursers; and at the far end a number of smoking kitchens. Finally, above the fountain, was a beautiful stone chapel, gracious and well constructed, that no-one had ever seen before. They all marvelled, saying that no one knew what might happen next, but anyhow it was a fine beginning, and please God that all would end well.

When the count and his suite descended the mount, an old knight, very elegantly dressed, with a belt studded with pearls and precious stones, mounted on a grey palfrey accompanied by a fine escort of twelve men, rode forward to greet them.

"My lord, my lady, Melusine of Scotland recommends herself to you, and thanks you for the great honour you have given to your cousin Raimondin and herself in coming to their wedding."

The count replied that he was much pleased, but did not think to find, so close to his domain, a lady of such high rank accompanied by such nobility.

They were shown to their tents. The Count's was the most sumptuous he had ever seen. The other lords were lodged according to their rank, and all said that they had never seen better in their own lands. The horses were kept in great tents, so spacious as to make things easy for the squires. And everyone wondered from where such wealth could come.

The Count's mother and his sister Blanche were installed in a tent embroidered with gold and precious stones so rich that all marvelled, and were received to the sound of melodious instruments.

Once rested and dressed, the countess and the ladies and maidens of her suite went to Melusine's tent, which was undoubtedly the most elegant of all. The beauty of the bride, her sumptuous finery and the richness of her clothes were marvellous to see. The countess herself said that she did not think that there existed in the world a queen, a king or an emperor whose riches equalled the value of the jewels that Melusine wore.

A bishop conducted the wedding service, which took place in the chapel, that was ornamented with fittings of strange and magnificent design, with gold embroidery and pearls of which no-one had ever seen the like before, together with statues, crosses, gold and silver thuribles, and gospels as precious as anyone could wish.

After the service they returned to the meadow, where a feast was served in a great and beautiful marquee. There was such an abundance of courses and such profusion of wines, that everyone asked from where it could all have come, and the speed and diligence of the servers was astonishing.

After the banquet, the tables were removed, grace said and several knights went to arm and mount their horses. The bride, the countess and her daughter took their places on a grandstand richly ornamented with cloth of gold, and the other ladies also. Then began a hot and eager joust in which the Count of Poitiers, the Count of Forez and the Poitevins accounted valiantly for themselves, but the knights of the bride also performed marvellously, striking horses and men to the ground.

Then Raimondin arrived incognito, mounted on a white horse richly caparisoned and harnessed in white that his lady had given him. On his first charge he overthrew the Count of Forez, his brother, and then comported himself so well that there was no knight on either side who sought to challenge him.

The young Count of Poitiers, curious to know who this knight was, put his shield before his chest, and galloped towards him, couching his lance. But Raimondin recognised him, and turned away, charging a knight of Poitou so forcefully that he was struck to the ground along with his horse. Raimondin's exploits were such that it was said that the knight in the white armour was the best jouster of the day.

When night came the tourney ended. The countess and the young bride returned to their tents to rest a little. Soon after, it was time to dine, and they all met in the great tent and were sumptuously served. After dinner, the tables were cleared and the ladies retired to put on shorter robes for dancing. The ball was very fine, with a great show of splendour, so that all marvelled at the illuminations and the luxury that surrounded them.

When the time came, they led the bride to bed, in a sumptuous tent erected next to the spring. The Countess of Poitiers and the other great ladies led her inside, and gave her their advice despite the fact that she did not lack for wisdom. She modestly thanked them for their counsel and then lay down, the ladies waiting around the bed chatting agreeably until Raimondin arrived, accompanied by the Count and his brother.

They led Raimondin into the tent and he lay down straight away, and the bishop who had married them arrived to bless the bed. Then all left and the curtains were drawn.

When everyone had gone and the flaps of the tent door had been secured, Melusine said to Raimondin: "My most dear lord, I thank you for the great honour that the people of your lineage have paid me today. I thank you too for having kept so well the secret of the promise that you made me at our first meeting. Be sure that if you hold to that promise, you will be the most powerful and honoured man of all your line. On the other hand, you and your descendants will suffer a great calamity the moment you betray your word about my presence on each seventh day – from which may God defend you."

"Do not worry, dear lady," replied Raimondin, "If it please God, it will never happen."

"My friend," said the lady, "after having promised me so much, I can only wait the will of God that you keep faith. Take care you do not fail, for apart from me, you will be the one who loses most."

"Madame," said Raimondin, "do not worry about that. May God abandon me the day I break your trust!"

"Then, my dear friend, let us speak no more of it. As for that which depends upon me, nothing will prevent me from making you, of all your line, a man most favoured by fortune and most powerful."

Then they ceased talking, and that night conceived their eldest son.

What else is there to say? The splendid feasting lasted for a fortnight; then the count, the countess, and all the barons took their leave. Melusine gave the countess a brooch of inestimable value, and to her daughter a diadem of pearls ornamented with sapphires, rubies, diamonds and other precious stones. Both brooch and the diadem dazzled all who saw them.

Melusine gave as much to the humble as to the great. All who came to the wedding were given rich presents, and left asking themselves from whence such riches could come, recognising that Raimondin had made a noble and powerful marriage.

When Raimondin returned from bidding farewell to his brother and to the count, he found another feast in progress, greater than the first. This in the presence of many strange guests who had been invited by Melusine, but all welcomed him and vowed that it was he whom they would now obey.

Very early next day Melusine took leave of her vassals, who went away, keeping with her only those she chose. Then she called in a great number of labourers and woodcutters whom she put to clearing the land and cleaning the face of the rock above the forest. She called in a crowd of masons and stoneworkers who began to construct massive foundations on the flattened rock.

They worked so fast and so well that those who passed by were stupified. Melusine paid them and provided them with bread, wine, meat and all their necessaries. What is more, no one knew from whence these workers came.

A fortress was very soon finished. Before getting to the keep one had to pass not one but two fortified places. The whole edifice was surrounded by powerful towers with battlements, and archers' vents within the walls. There were three pairs of advance walls, very high and very strong, furnished with many towers and solid postern gates. On the side of the fortress that overlooked the high forest, the rock above the meadow was so steep that no one could climb it. They even cut advanced walls out of the rock. The fortress was thus incredibly strong and all were amazed to see how little time it took to build.

The Count of Poitiers declared it the most beautiful and powerful fortification he had ever seen, and asked Melusine to give it a name. Whereupon she called it Lusignan, and this name was proclaimed throughout the country. Here Melusine and Raimondin settled in as its rich and powerful lord and lady.

Melusine also built the town of Lusignan, and a great high tower between town and citadel so that watchmen could see all around and sound their trumpets when anyone approached, and so it was called the trumpet tower.

In that first year she also built the château and town of Ainnelle, as well as Vouvant and Mervent, and then the town and tower of St. Maixent where she also began the construction of the abbey. She also did a great deal for the poor.

In later years she built many more strong places in the county of Poitou and duchy of Guyenne, including the château and town of Parthenay, of a strength and beauty without equal. At La Rochelle she built the château and coast guard towers as well as part of the town. Three leagues from there Julius Caesar had built a tower called the Tower of the Eagle on account of the imperial eagle that he carried on his banner. Melusine built other great towers around this tower and called the château Aiglon. Then she built Talmont and Talmondois, and many other towns and fortresses, and Raymond acquired such land developed from virgin forest that there was no prince in Brittany, Guyenne or Poitou who could rival him.

Many years passed and Raymondin and Melusine had ten sons. Some of them had distinguished careers as knightly champions. The four eldest worked in pairs rescuing heiresses from usurping tyrants. They thus gained lands through the sovereignty of the maidens whom they saved.

The fifth son, Geoffrey, was a wild and solitary one, living on the verges of the civilised world. He followed out the pattern of a warrior hero, which included killing giants. He was also nicknamed Great Tooth, for he had a protruding tooth like the tusk of a boar, and was capable of a bestial fury, when his face would become suffused with blood and he would froth at the mouth like a boar.

During all her years of marriage and bearing and rearing her sons, Melusine continued to draw apart and hide herself every Saturday. Faithful to his promise, Raymondin never sought to see her on this day or tried to penetrate her secret.

Until one ill-fated Saturday he received a visit from his brother, the Count of Forez, who asked why Melusine was not present, as he particularly wished to speak with her. But Raimondin replied that she could not be seen, and would not be back until the morrow. Instead of being satisfied, the Count of Forez revealed the real cause of his visit. He told his brother that there were tales that his wife had wronged his reputation, that on this day she was indulging in secret debauchery.

Raimondin had never imagined this of his wife, but at the thought a great rage overcome him and he took up a sword and rushed to Melusine's quarters. He found his way barred by a heavy door but in his anguish he turned and twisted the point of his sword until he had made a hole through which he could see.

There he saw Melusine. She was naked, bathing in a great marble pool, and combing her hair, but below the waist she had an enormous tail with blue and silver scales with which she struck the water so that it splashed up to the height of the walls.

Raimond was desolated, and realised he had broken his word. Cursing the evil counsel of his brother, he ran from the chamber back to the great hall. His brother saw his distress and assumed he had discovered the guilt of his wife.

"There you are!" he said "Now have you seen what I warned you about?"

"Get out of here, base traitor!" Raimondin cried. "By your infernal lies you have made me foreswear the best of wives, and the most faithful in the world. You have brought grief upon me, destroyed all my joy. Oh God, if I had only looked in my own heart. I would strike you down if you were not my own brother. Go! Get out of my sight and may all the servants of hell go with you!"

Seeing his brother had almost lost his reason, the Count left the hall, and galloped back to Forez, greatly distressed at losing Raimondin's affection, who indeed refused to see him ever again.

Raimondin went to his room and lay on the bed, full of despair, striking his breast and tearing at his face. He remained in a state of misery through to the small hours of the morning.

When dawn came Melusine entered the room and he pretended to be asleep as she undressed and lay down beside him. When the time came they arose and went to mass. Then breakfast was served and so passed the day. The next day after, Melusine left for Niort where she was building a great fortress with twin towers.

As she said nothing about his intrusion, Raimondin thought she might not know about what had occurred. In this he was wrong; she knew all, but as he had not spoken to anyone about it, she made as if nothing had happened.

Not long afterwards news came to him of trouble with two of their sons. Fromont had become a religious at the abbey of Maillezais, and Geoffrey, the wild one and reputed killer of giants, had entered into such madness that he had set fire to the chapterhouse, burned the abbot and monks inside and even half the abbey.

Raimondin left at a furious gallop to Maillezais without waiting for an escort. When he saw the extent of the catastrophe his heart burned to think that his son, of such renown in valour and honour, had completely destroyed it by his cruelty. He recalled the sight of Melusine in the form of a serpent from the waist down. He recalled the great boar that had caused him to kill his uncle and the boar tusk in his son's mouth. He recalled the odd birth marks of others of his sons, with displaced or disproportionate eyes or ears, or patches of fur on the face. Then he asked himself if he had not married some evil spirit, or an apparition, or an illusion that had abused him, the fruit of whose womb could never bring forth good.

He rode on to Mervent where he alighted, went to a room and threw himself down, cursing the day that Geoffrey had been born and even she who had given birth to him. The lords, touched by his torment, seeing they could not calm him, decided to call Melusine.

The messenger arrived at Niort, saluted the lady and gave her the letter that the barons had sent. She took it, broke the seal and read it, and was filled with consternation. She then left Niort but went to Lusignan, where she spent two days, walking through the castle from top to bottom, visiting places she had known, crying out from time to time and deeply sighing. It seems that she knew the misfortune that was coming to her. But those there at the time could not imagine that and thought the cause of her distress to be that Geoffrey had killed his brother and the monks.

But she was more concerned about Raimondin, for she saw that nothing could be done for the moment about the wrong that Geoffrey had done. On the third day she left Lusignan and went to Mervent with her ladies and entered the room where Raimondin lay. The room gave onto pleasant gardens and the fields beyond. She greeted Raimondin lovingly but he was so afflicted that he made no response.

She spoke to him, trying to comfort him, saying it folly to show such despair over something that could not be changed and for which there was no remedy. He surely knew there was no sinner, however great, to whom God would not show mercy at sincere repentance. If their son had committed this crime by the violence of his feelings may it not have been because of the sins of the monks, leading a life of debauchery and disorder? The Lord might have wished to punish them, through Geoffrey, for some unknown cause, for the ways of God are mysterious to men.

On the other hand, were she and Raimondin not rich enough to rebuild the abbey more beautiful that it was before? To grant it a generous endowment? To put more monks there than ever there were before? Geoffrey would mend his ways, if it pleased God and nature. For all these reasons she begged her husband to stop grieving.

Raimondin realised that what she said was true, and for the most part undeniable, but he was so transported with fury that all good sense had left him. He thus spoke to her cruelly:

"Oh infamous serpent, in the name of God, go! You and your deeds are no more than an illusion. Can those who were burnt to death be brought back to life? They have been destroyed by a demon, for all who fall madly furious are ruled by the princes of Hell. That is why Geoffrey committed this hideous crime, burning the monks and his brother."

The words caused Melusine such pain that she fell into a swoon. For over half an hour she remained, with imperceptible breathing and a non-existent pulse. Raimondin became yet more despairing than before. His fury calmed at a stroke, and he was overcome with grief. He now regretted his words, but that served no purpose. It was too late.

The lords and ladies, in consternation, gathered round, sprinkling their lady's face with cold water, and finally restored her to her senses. When she could speak, she looked long and deeply at Raimondin and said:

"Ah Raimondin, the day I saw you for the first time was an evil day for me. Alas, it was to my misfortune that I saw your grace, your youth, your beauty. It is my misfortune that I desired your love and now you have so ignobly betrayed me.

"Even though you broke your promise, I forgave you from the bottom of my heart, for you had spoken to no-one about it. And God would have forgiven you, because you were so penitent.

"Alas, my friend, now your love has changed to hate, your tenderness to cruelty. Our pleasures and our joys have turned to tears and crying, our good fortune to misfortune and calamity.

"Alas, if you had not betrayed me, I would have been saved from my pain and torment. I would have lived a natural course of life, as a normal woman. I would have died naturally, with all the sacraments of the church. I would have been buried in the church of Notre Dame of Lusignan and memorial masses would have been said for me.

"But now you have plunged me back into the punishment that I have long suffered because of my fault. And this I must now bear until the Day of Judgement, because you have betrayed me. I pray that God may forgive you."

And she showed such grief that no heart in the world would not have been softened.

Seeing this, Raimondin himself was overwhelmed, so that he saw no more, heard no more, understood no more. But when he regained his wits a little and saw Melusine before him, he knelt, clasping her hands saying:

"My dear love, my dear, my hope and my honour, I beg you, in the name of the sufferings of Jesus Christ, and in the same glorious forgiveness that the true son of God accorded to Mary Magdalene, of your good will to forgive me this fault and to stay with me."

"My tender love," said Melusine, who saw the torrents of tears pouring from his eyes, "may He from whom flows all mercy pardon your fault. As for me, I forgive you with all my heart. But as for that which must come to pass, the Sovereign Lord ordained it so."

At these words she held him in her arms, embracing him with such sadness that all present began to weep in sympathy. She raised Raimondin up and sat him beside her and said:

"Listen to what I say to you. My dear husband, know that I can no longer remain with you, God wills it so because of your fault. That is why I must now speak to you and to all who wait upon you."

"My sweet love," said Raimondin, "we will not fail you. But in the name of God, and for pity's sake, do not dishonour me completely. Stay, or my heart will never again know joy."

She replied: "My dear friend, if it were in my power to do so, then I would. But it is impossible. Know that I suffer a hundred thousand times more grief than you by our separation. But so it must be, because He who can do and undo all things, has so decreed."

At these words, she took him again in her arms and embraced him very tenderly saying: "Farewell, my most sweet love, my good, my heart and all my joy. Know that for as long as you live, I will continue to be able to see you, even though, once I have left, you will never more see me in human form."

Then she jumped onto the sill of one of the windows that gave onto the countryside around.

Standing at the window, she took her leave, gazing sadly at Raimondin and all there present, crying so bitterly that everyone pitied her. Then she turned her eyes to the country outside, saying:

"Ah, sweet country, you have given me such joy and pleasure. I could have found my happiness in you if God had not willed that I should be so terribly betrayed. Alas, the people of this country look upon me as their lady, and would do anything I asked. Now I can never live here, even as a poor chambermaid. Those who greeted me with such joy would now fly in fear of me, I would strike horror into those that saw me. All the joys that I found will become pain and suffering, penitence and despondency."

Then she added, raising her voice: "I commend each and every one of you to God. Pray to Our Lord that He will be pleased to lighten my punishment. I want you to know that I am, as was my father, like unto you. Do not reproach my children with being the sons of a bad mother, or a faery or a serpent. I am the daughter of King Helias of Scotland and Queen Pressine, his wife. We were three sisters to whom has been assigned a cruel destiny, a terrible punishment. And I cannot – nor want to – say any more to you of that."

Then with a most dolorous cry she leaped into the air, out of the window, and passed above the orchard, turning into a great winged serpent some fifteen feet long. And the stone from which she jumped from the window still has the form of her foot imprinted upon it.

Then great dole came to the lords and ladies, and the maidens who had personally served her. They went to the windows to see which way she was going. They saw her, in the form of a serpent, fly three times round the fortress. Each time she passed she gave a cry so strange and dolorous that everyone wept with pity, seeing she was leaving against her will, forced and constrained to do so.

Then she made her way towards Lusignan. The country people were amazed, seeing her flying in the air above them, making such cries, together with a humming and a roaring as if a thunderstorm or tempest were about to come upon them.

When she came to Lusignan she circled it three times, crying most piteously, lamenting with a human voice, so that those in the fortress and the town were amazed. They knew not what to think as they saw the figure of a serpent and heard the voice of a woman coming from it.

Then, when she had flown round the fort three times, she landed on the Poitevin tower so violently, and with such a noise of storm, that it seemed to all who lived within that the whole building might fall, as all the stones within it moved one against the other.

She stayed for some time on the Poitevin tower, and then seeing her two youngest children crying was so grieved that she gave such a prodigious cry that it seemed as if the fortress must tumble. Then she cried more quietly. Finally, she rose into the air and flew away towards Aragon, her tail trailing behind her, unbelievably long and of blue and silver scales.

That same day she appeared at Montserrat, where the prior and monks saw her. Then, suddenly, she disappeared, and no-one knew where she had gone.

One of the barons present when Melusine made her departure said that she proclaimed that she would reappear if ever the fortress was about to have a change of master. And also, whenever one of Raimondin's descendants died – either at Lusignan or at the place of death.

Such is the story of Melusine as it has been passed down from mouth to ear through generations of the Lusignans, and later rendered into written chronicle by a clerkly hand.

Chapter Three

⁕

Images of Melusine

HERE are several layers of meaning and interpretation in any medieval romance when it is based upon or influenced by ancient oral material. The best way to cope with this multilevel awareness is to treat it visually, almost as a strip cartoon, in a series of iconic images. These meditational pictures represent key steps in the unfolding of the story, but also, as with any valid esoteric glyph, can stand alone as gateways to wisdom and experience in their own right. In this respect a picture is worth a thousand words, an emotive one worth more! As iconic images they can be gateways to another world.

If we break up the romance of Melusine and Raimondin in this fashion we can come up with a sequence such as the following. It not the only possible one, for there is room for individual emphasis and personal preference.

1. Raimondin is presented at court.
2. The boar hunt.
3. The clearing in the forest.
4. The death of the boar and Count Aymeri.
5. Raimondin carried through the forest by his horse.
6. The faeries at the fountain.
7. The pact of Melusine and Raimondin.
8. At the gates of Poitiers, the bodies of the boar and Count Aymeri brought in.
9. Raymondin asks the new Count of Poitiers for land.
10. Measuring out the land and the rising of a spring.
11. Arrangements for the wedding.
12. The wedding of Melusine and Raimondin.
13. Melusine sends Raimondin to Brittany.
14. Melusine builds the town and castle of Lusignan.
15. Melusine equips her elder sons for conquest and adventure.
16. Raimondin's brother sows seeds of doubt.

17. Melusine in her serpent form.
18. The reconciliation of Melusine and Raimondin.
19. The murder of Fromont.
20. Raimondin denounces Melusine.
21. Melusine's farewell.
22. Melusine's return.

This is enough to be going on with. It covers the main sequence of the story, and we will pursue various branches of the story later, concerning the various sons of Melusine, her sisters and parents. But this is the main stem from which all else derives.

There is no substitute for building the images in the mind. It brings them closer to the field of our own personal experience, which in turn can produce deeper realisations. This is the direct opposite of intellectual speculation.

An intellectual approach is the bugbear of any who seek to come to terms with evocative images of myth and legend. It is a particular problem for academic researchers, limited as they are by their discipline to rational analysis. The images need to be experienced, not explained.

This applies equally to the esoteric diagrams of alchemists and Rosicrucians at a later stage in tradition. Images were often not put there to illustrate a text. They *are* the text.

Verbal explanations can thus be something of a distraction from what is more plainly presented by picture, story and emotive engagement. The notes that follow are therefore not intended to be a substitute for imaginative participation. But rather as supplementary material that may help to oil the hinges of the gateways to inner experience.

1. Raimondin is presented at court.
Raimondin comes to the court of Count Aymeri of Poitiers on account of being his nephew, the son of the Countess's brother. This was very much the custom and practice of noble families. A young man would be placed with another branch of the family to be brought up and trained as page and squire before winning his spurs as a knight.

Celtic inheritance tended to be matrilinear, and we note that it is through his aunt, his mother's sister, that Raimondin is taken into the court at Poitiers. This suggests we are dealing with material that comes from Celtic legend rather than contemporary social custom.

It is thus no surprise to find a strong tie between the two in the story. Count Aymeri looks upon Raimondin almost as a son, and Raimondin looks up to the count as a sage and hero. They become close companions, and their fates are inextricably linked – even surrogates for one another.

2. The boar hunt.

The motif of a hunt, and particularly a boar hunt, is, in Celtic mythology, the prelude to entry into the Otherworld. This boar happens to be a particularly large and ferocious one. So much so, that the rest of the hunters fear to go near it, and it despatches any hunting hounds that try.

It is only when Count Aymeri spurs up and jibes them all for their cowardice that Raimondin makes a first foray at it, which is the cause (and indeed signal) for the magical animal to turn and rush off into the forest. It is an Otherworld lure for the two of them.

The rest of the hunt are soon left behind, as Raimondin and Count Aymeri, wound up by the excitement of the hunt, pursue it all day through the forest.

The forest also represents the Otherworld and is the place where faeries abide along with many another strange creature. As Charles Williams has remarked about the magical forest of Broceliande, it is a place for lovers, poets or lunatics – and of course questing knights – and no one comes out of it unchanged!

3. The clearing in the forest.

The boar having eluded them, Raimondin and Count Aymeri find themselves lost and alone as darkness gathers. In the forest clearing the stage is set for the mystery that is about to come upon them.

Count Aymeri gazes at the stars – not simply in wonder but because he is a skilled astrologer, and the stars are about to reveal their impending destiny.

Raimondin sets about lighting a fire, which has more than utilitarian significance if we take account, as Dr. Morris suggests, that this hunt may well have taken place at Samhain, a festival that marks the turn of the Celtic year, celebrated by the lighting of fires. It is the time when the old god gives place to the new.

This gives a deeper significance to the message that Count Aymeri declares he has seen in the stars – that if a young vassal should kill his lord at this time he will go on to great success and to found a dynasty. Viewed in purely secular terms this seems to Raimondin both a horror and an impossibility, but there are greater forces at play than this young man dreams of.

4. The death of the boar and Count Aymeri.

No sooner has Count Aymeri described this eventuality than, as if on cue, the great boar reappears. It rushes to attack, and in the resulting mêlée Raimondin kills both boar and the Count – indeed with the same spear thrust. This further suggests that the boar and the Count represent the same dynamic – the old god whose death is brought about by the new. Raimondin is taking on the archetypal role of Mabon – the "Great Son" of Modron, the "Great Mother" in Celtic myth.

5. Raimondin carried through the forest by his horse.

Raimondin is a complete innocent, in much the same way as Perceval in the Graal stories. And seeing things only at the surface level, of having killed his lord, albeit by chance, it seems to him that his whole life is in ruins, that he is destined to become no more than a fugitive and outlaw – an outsider in every sense of the word. Completely distraught, he mounts his horse and leaves the scene, not caring where he goes, and allows the animal to take him where it will.

In terms of the archetypal dynamics behind the story, we might recall the significance of the horse in Celtic myth. It is identified with the goddess in her aspect of Epona. She is about to take him to her own. Nor is it a coincidence that the full moon has risen high into the sky. An epiphany of the goddess is likely to be at hand.

At another level the role of the horse attunes with the doctrine of the Three-fold Alliance, (described in R.J. Stewart's *The Living World of Faery* and *Earth Light)*, the required restitution of the link between the human, the animal, and the faery worlds. Here the horse is the intermediary between human and faery.

6. The faeries at the fountain.

The three faeries dancing in the moonlight at the fountain by the rocks is at one level an appearance of the Three-fold Goddess –

as she reveals herself in all her glory and beauty to the New God hero after the slaughter of the Old One.

For the purposes of the story the leading figure is the faery Melusine. Whether her two companions are her sisters, or simply aspects of herself, is open to conjecture. The possibilities are not mutually exclusive.

Raimondin cannot see them at first. In the story it is put down to his fatigue although it may also accord with the need to re-attune his vision from human to faery levels of perception. Until now a normal human youth concerned entirely with the physical world about him of court and field, he is suddenly opened up to contact with the Otherworld.

Another element may be his psychological condition. He has fallen into almost a cataleptic state from which he needs awakening. Did this state of psychological trauma help to bring this opening up of vision? In some other accounts of faeries making themselves known, the hero is in a state of suffering or loss, such as grieving the death of a wife.

Faeries appearing at a fountain are relatively commonplace in folklore, which accounts for the many grottoes in Catholic countries graced with statues of the Virgin Mary or by minor saints. The original incumbent was probably a faery and indeed might still be, quite content with her new guise!

The symbolism of rising waters of life from the earth is much in accord with their function.

7. The pact of Melusine and Raimondin.

With Raimondin's disillusionment with the physical world the possibility of help from the inner worlds opens up for him. This is an experience that comes to many people. It is the process of the "Seeker" in esoteric tradition and indeed for many who are called to a religious faith. It requires giving allegiance, even unreserved dedication, to an inner world teacher or guide.

As in all things this can be open to abuse. The cautionary tale of Dr. Faustus seeking power and forbidden knowledge by bartering his soul to Mephistopheles is cited as a dreadful example. The inner worlds are very extensive and all kinds of beings may be found there, so Dr Faustus remains a good example of what not to do. It seems akin to doing a deal with the Mafia on the physical plane. They may well deliver the goods for a certain period but they drive a hard bargain when it comes to payback time! No doubt there are as many fools, humbugs and plausible tricksters on the inner planes as on the outer, so we need to choose a guide with care. Here much depends on motive.

Raimondin is patently an innocent, and victim of some cruel and atrocious circumstances, and is at first inclined simply to rail against a cruel and irrational Fate. At some deep level he may be acting out a role in some archetypal drama of group dynamics but he is in no condition to understand that! He has not gone into the woods in search of faeries to provide him with sexual favours along with wealth and power. Rather, the faery has come to him, seeking his partnership in a work of mutual destiny.

The world of faery is quite close to the physical world but it is no bad thing because of that. Indeed tradition has it that the Inner Earth contains the pattern of the Earthly Paradise – whether we regard this as a past or a future condition, or even pertaining to both. Tolkien has come close to providing a vision of this in *The Silmarillion* in the creation and evolution of the elven, human and other kingdoms in his great visionary fantasy. But his vision is not the only window into this darkly splendid world.

We are, at any rate, now on fairly well trodden ground of faery contacts with human beings, and of a mating between the two. This can happen in two ways; either the human is taken off into the faery world, perhaps never to be seen again, or the faery takes on a garment of flesh to appear as a human being – usually one of superlative beauty, wisdom and remarkable powers. Laurence Harf-Lancner, a leading academic authority on faery lore, has classified these respectively as a "Morgan type" and a "Melusine type".

In the latter case a particular condition is imposed upon the human being, generally known as a *geas*, the breaking of which involves the faery returning to her original state. Whilst this may seem totally irrational, there might be a very real need for the faery to return to a non-human form from time to time (a chance to recharge her batteries, so to speak) for she is operating for the most part in an alien element and environment.

This certainly seems a lot more reasonable than the assumption in the original romance, which we will come to later, that it is all the result of a vindictive curse laid on her by her mother Pressine.

Why a Saturday should be chosen for the day set apart is not revealed but there are several possibilities. Saturday is the original Sabbath and the day that Christ entered the Underworld at the first Easter – which according to one tradition included taking his mission to the faery kingdoms. So Melusine, who claims to be and always acts like a devout Christian, might find this day to have a particularly commemorative significance, along with returning to the human condition on Sunday morning, Resurrection Day.

Saturday has also been the day set apart by the Catholic church to honour the Virgin, which suggests an association of the feminine principle with this day even in most orthodox circles. Whatever! The important point is whether or not Raimondin manages to observe her privacy or not. It is, in its ultimate sense, a test of faith and love and mutual respect expressed over time – the *sine qua non* of any successful marital relationship – which applies equally in any exchange of vows between human and faery.

8. At the gates of Poitiers, the bodies of the boar and Count Aymeri brought in.

Having agreed to plight his troth to the faery in return for her guidance, Raimondin's first task is to follow her instructions, going back to the city and swearing ignorance of the recent occurrences. This is also something of a test of faith, in fact the first of three, of trust in the wisdom of his faery guide in knowing what best to do, and obedience in keeping silent.

This is encapsulated in the scene where he waits with others at the gates of the city as the body of the Count is borne home together with the body of the boar. That the boar is being burnt outside the church where the funerary rites of the Count are observed, again suggests that boar and Count are symbolically as one – the old god and his totemic representative.

9. Raymondin asks the new Count of Poitiers for land.

There is a series of comings and goings of Raimondin between the court of Poitiers and Melusine at the fountain, which represents a kind of polar interchange between the powers of the outer and the inner.

Having proven that he can obey instructions and keep a secret, Raimondin is entrusted with more complex and constructive tasks. This is very much the pattern for an initiate in the world, having made contact with a responsible inner plane mentor. This sequence of seeking rights of land, more complicated than his last set of instructions, is the second test.

As Melusine has instructed, Raimondin has to ask the Count and his barons for this grant of land in acknowledgment of "past services" to the old count. We are well aware of the deeper significance of these "services" as part of an ancient ritual drama between old and new god, though they are beyond the ken of both Raimondin and the lords.

The request is apparently so insignificant that it is it readily granted, ratified with many seals, and complete freehold is thrown in as well – an unheard of situation in feudal times. In later family history tradition this was the root of the Lusignan family's boast not to bow the knee to any overlord, which suggests that the faery legend was in the family for some considerable time.

The whole process demonstrates the faery Melusine's detailed and subtle knowledge of the thought processes and customs of the world of men. As wise as she is beautiful – and shrewdly practical with it!

Having gained the principle of the gift of land the next step is to determine its size and location. Here Raimondin has to purchase the deerskin from a man Melusine predicts he will meet, without haggling over the price – a formula often met with in medieval magical practice. Then it must be cut in a certain complicated way. All this may have been beyond the comprehension of Raimondin but he does as he is told.

The device of cutting up a skin so as to make it into a very long ball of leather thread, is, however, not original to Melusine. The legendary queen Dido used a similar device to obtain land upon which to build the city of Carthage. This is recounted by Virgil in the *Aenead*, which was favoured classical reading by medieval clerks but seems not to have been well known to the lords of Poitou at the time of Melusine!

10. Measuring out the land and the rising of a spring.

The Count's surveyors are nonplussed to see how the deer skin has been transformed into a very lengthy skein, and are puzzled about what to do with it. Practical faery help is however at hand. Two mysterious strangers appear out of the woods and take over the task, outlining the bounds of what is to become the domain of Lusignan.

Their progress is accompanied by the miraculous rising of a spring that later becomes a stream large enough to drive watermills. Plainly Melusine has great plans for the site. In prosaic terms the stream could perhaps be identified with the Bourceron, which runs today from the Font-de-Cé along the length of the town of Lusignan to debouch into the River Vonne a little upstream – although in the romance it appears to be a separate spring from the fountain at which Melusine first appeared.

11. Arrangements for the wedding.

At his third meeting with Melusine, Raimondin is hoping for a quick consummation of her promised love with the minimum of ceremony but she now reveals that their marriage is to be no hole-and-corner private affair. She tells him to invite the Count of Poitiers along with all his vassals to the event, which surprisingly is to take place here in the forest, and even more surprisingly in a very few days. This seems a bizarre and complete impossibility but nonetheless Raimondin sets off in good faith to perform his task.

This is his third and final test and no small one, for Raimondin is putting himself at considerable risk. Apart from the seeming unlikelihood of the event ever taking place, it was his duty, as a close relative of the Count, not only to seek permission to marry, but to allow his lord to select the bride. Marriage was a serious matter of dynastic interest and political diplomacy – not of personal whim or affections.

Fortunately for Raimondin the Count is willing to overlook this lapse of protocol but he assumes that Raimondin must have selected an appropriate bride from a well connected noble family. To his amazement Raimondin cannot even tell him the bride's name!

This is a shocking state of affairs. So bizarre in fact that the Count seems quite disarmed when Raimondin points out that if he has chosen wrongly, he is the one who will have to live with the consequences. There is no disputing his logic but he was nonetheless putting himself at great risk had the Count been less accommodating. Vassals have been imprisoned or exiled for less. However, it seems that Melusine, in her wisdom, had taken all this into account.

12. The wedding of Melusine and Raimondin

When all the guests arrive they are amazed at what they see laid out before them. Part of the forest has been cleared (an essential mark of progress in early medieval times), and a vast array of tents and pavilions erected, remarkable for their luxurious appointment. Never has the like been seen before, and the Count's concerns about the suitability of Raimondin's match are blown away, not only by the scale and splendour of the feast, but Melusine's announcement that she is the daughter of a king and queen, Helias and Pressine of Albany. This considerably outranks the Count himself!

The quality and amount of riches on display seem proof that this is no empty claim. There is a vast array of servants to wait upon the needs of the guests, presumably of the faery kind, for they are extremely speedy and efficient. The powers of faery are beginning to manifest in the land.

In the rites of sacred kingship in Celtic lands, which underpins the story of Raimondin and Melusine, two elements predominate. One is a generous libation of wine and general feasting and games, which are here in abundance, regaled at almost tedious length in the original romance.

The other element is sexual, here with the ritual bedding of the couple. This is more or less according to contemporary custom although we may note that the nuptial tent is placed close by the fountain where Melusine first appeared. This may not be for merely sentimental reasons.

It is also the occasion for a little pillow talk, and some gentle admonition from Melusine, perhaps with a preview of the future, or an awareness of the frailty of men, about the importance of remaining faithful to the vow he has given, to allow her withdrawal from the world for one day of each week.

After which, in keeping with medieval convention, on the first night of their marriage they conceive the first of their sons.

13. Melusine sends Raimondin to Brittany.

Rather surprisingly, soon after the wedding Melusine sends Raimondin off on a military expedition. There seems to be more than one purpose in this, and it is indeed a feature of many an inner plane guide that in their actions they contrive to kill several birds with one stone. In this instance the objective seems threefold.

Raimondin is given a chance to prove himself as a knight, and we should remember that he is still somewhat of a callow youth, possibly still only a squire in the old Count's service.

The second is to restore the reputation of his father, Hervé de Leon, the detail of which we shall examine later, of which Melusine seems to have a more than passing interest and knowledge that she does not fully reveal.

Thirdly, and perhaps most importantly, she uses the time that Raimondin is away to build of the town of Lusignan and its castle.

Back of all this is the mythopoeic subtext of the story. Raimondin is being schooled to take the place of the old lord he killed at the start of the Celtic new year, one of the paramount functions of which is to set wrongs to rights and to maintain justice.

14. Melusine builds the town and castle of Lusignan.
Melusine is not only a faery bride, she is an embodiment of the sovereignty of the land over which Raimondin now rules, and to which he is formally wedded. From what was at first bare rock near a forest fountain, a town and castle springs up, which was in keeping with the general thrust of human civilisation at that time. Wild forest covered most of Europe and modern civilisation only developed after it had been cleared and rendered suitable for crops and herds and the growth of towns.

There has been much speculation as to whether Melusine took her name from Lusignan or the town took its name from her. According to the romance, it was she who named the town, at the request of the Count of Poitiers, who approved her choice for two reasons. Her name was Melusine of Albany, and Albany in Greek meant "that which is faultless", whilst Melusine meant "marvellous". Whether or not his etymology is accurate the Count's admiration for her and her feats of construction is obvious. She has obviously won complete acceptance in the human world.

More recent etymological buffs have likened the name Melusine to the evergreen oaks that grow in Poitou called "l'yeuse" or "l'eusine", and thus wonder if she was originally a dryad or an oak tree goddess.

Another theory has been that Melusine derives from the goddess Lucina, who in ancient times presided over childbirth and over crossroads, for Lusignan is a crossroads of sorts, in that the road from Poitiers divides here, one to go the pilgrim route to Santiago de Compostella and the other to the port of La Rochelle.

Locals tended to call her Merlusine – which has led to speculation that this derives from Mère (mother) Lusine. This popular tradition would link her with an ancient feminine figure who flew round the country at night carrying great stones for building operations, some of which she dropped from her apron by accident, and which formed what we now regard as ancient megaliths and Roman ruins. This figure of popular folklore, it should be said, has also been identified with a local saint, St Radegonde, as well as Melusine. Actually, much of the construction work throughout Poitou attributed to Melusine was 12th century work of the Plantagenets, particularly Eleanor of Aquitaine.

However, there is a deep stratum of legend, particularly with regard to subterranean building operations, including an alleged underground passage through the chalk linking Lusignan with Poitiers.

At the lowest level of popular belief and superstition Melusine has been linked, at least by name, to various wild tales. Some invented or embroidered by clerics associating faery belief with evil spirits. Others at a more domestic level of threatening children with a bogey figure if they do not behave.

15. Melusine equips her elder sons for conquest and adventure.
Above all, in the romance, Melusine was a prolific mother, particularly of sons, which was a medieval ideal of the warrior class. We have not taken the trouble to recount the adventures of the elder sons, for they are more in the nature of *chansons de geste* – action adventure and war tales – with little connection to mythical dynamics. They are for the most part misremembered fragments of family history or attempts to link Lusignan with important dynasties. They also formed useful instruction books on the arts of contemporary warfare (that is to say 14th century warfare, when the romance was written) not only with bloody details of personal combat but the organisation of armies and strategic plans in the field. This added to the popularity of the romance in the later middle ages.

16. Raimondin's brother sows seeds of doubt.

Ever since Cain and Abel, family conflict has been a deep seated part of the human condition. It is also a feature in many tales of alliances between human beings and those of the faery kind. It is a member of the human's family who sows the seeds of discord – of distrust in "the other".

In this case it is a brother, the Count of Forez, although in the famous tale of Cupid and Psyche, it is Psyche's envious sisters who sow seeds of discord, leading Psyche to betray the God of Love. In other tales of faery marriages to human beings it may be the hero's mother who takes on this evil role, as in the story of the Swan Knights, where it was the king's mother who sought to destroy the faery's seven children.

There is the tendency to suspect the worst of things we do not understand, along with a natural dissociation of workaday family ties from the influx of the otherworldly or the miraculous. Even Jesus was not taken seriously when he tried to preach in his own home town. They could see him only as a local carpenter's son.

17. Melusine in her serpent form.

This is one of the key images of the whole romance. It was a popular one with the woodcut artists of the early printed editions and has remained so, if only to show a faery lady in a state of undress, or even as part of a freak show.

But beyond that there is a realisation of the human condition on Raimondin's part. Of attempting to discover truth of the unknown, of forbidden secrets, which must have puzzled him mightily over the years. It is therefore a scene full of human drama on a general as well as a personal level, upon which the whole fate of Raimondin and Melusine is at risk.

Melusine seems quite happy to be back in what is presumably her own element, as she lies combing her hair and threshing the water with her tail. This does not necessarily mean that she is no more than a water sprite. Nor does she seem a mermaid as some antiquarians have been inclined to describe her, for it is not a fish's tail she has but a serpent's. So if water is her element it seems definitely to be fresh rather than salt. She is a being of the inland woods and streams and lakes, the virgin land itself, rather than a sea creature.

Much ink has been expended in speculation about her possible serpentine origins. In earlier tales retailed by Gervais of Tilbury and others, the faery has been depicted as a dragon, in one instance rather like a destructive dog chewing up the carpet! Melusine's tail however seems to be a thing of beauty, glistening in bands of blue and silver – the colours of the Lusignan arms.

Harking back to the story of Adam and Eve in the Garden of Eden, fundamentalist exegesis tends to see nothing but menace, seduction and evil in the serpentine form. However, there is another side to this. It could be that the advice of the serpent was a way of advancing humanity from a static condition – as limited in potential as the angels – to become as gods (to quote God's remark) if at considerable cost through "the knowledge of good and of evil". In ancient lore the serpent was seen as a symbol of wisdom – but it obviously comes at a price.

At a local level Melusine's serpentine association may originate in Celtic or pre-Celtic mythology. The Poitiers region was occupied by a Roman legion of Scythes who had a serpent goddess in their pantheon. Likewise the Celts, who had a tribal capital here, held a ram-headed serpent to be a symbol of fruitfulness.

However, as we said before, intellectual speculation is not likely to get us very far. Rather than take in other people's intellectual washing it may be better to simply fix our gaze on Melusine and, like Raimondin, accept her for what she is. After all he did not run to the library to try and find a book about it!

Rather, Raimondin's first realisation of the truth about his faery bride was one of tenderness and self reproach at his own conduct. Whatever condemnation he felt was directed at his brother for his evil saying. Although at another level this is a projection onto the Count of Forez of his own guilt for believing the weasel words. Hence he sends his brother packing.

18. The reconciliation of Raimondin and Melusine.

This is one of the most moving scenes in the romance, as Raimondin who has been in a desolation of grief all night is comforted by Melusine as she returns at dawn on Sunday morning to join him in their bed.

It is also something of a revelation, as we, along with Raimondin, realise that all can be forgiven insofar that he has kept his knowledge of Melusine's secret to himself. The bond of mutual trust may have been broken, but it has not been revealed to the world.

There are deeper moral issues involved, depending upon the reasons for her serpentine form and need to keep it secret, as described in another part of the romance. We will consider these when we deal with the faery kin of Melusine.

19. The murder of Fromont.

This is where the romance of Melusine and Raimondin comes hard up against the action story of their famous son Geoffrey Great-tooth. The murder of the innocent monks, and of their son Fromont, in an act of savage fratricide that is later compounded when Geoffrey, not content with his father having banished the Count of Forez, seeks nothing less than his uncle's death in revenge. These again are matters best dealt with later when we examine the character and story of Geoffrey in some detail. The crucial element here is in Raimondin's reaction.

20. Raimondin denounces Melusine.

Geoffrey's fratricidal act is the breaking point as far as Raimondin is concerned. He must, over the years, have had, at the back of his mind at least, a puzzled concern over the strange deformations of most of their sons, despite their otherwise laudable characteristics, and in particular the monstrosity called Horrible who was the eighth to be born.

Taking up the conventional priestly approach to the faerie kingdom of regarding it as demonic, Raimondin publicly denounces Melusine as a fiend and serpent. *"Ah, false serpent! By God, thou and all of thy actions are naught but sorcery!"*

What a depth of human misunderstanding, weakness, fear, rejection and condemnation are encapsulated in this cry!

21. Melusine's farewell.

This latest event is not only a breaking of Raimondin's trust and resolve, but of the union between human and faery worlds. Things are now well beyond the power of Melusine to forgive and forget. The whole world has been let into her secret and she has been denounced by her husband in the most unequivocal of terms. It brings about her complete and public transformation, to a kind of dragon woman, not only with the blue and silver serpent tail but with bat wings and clawed feet as well.

After tender exchanges of regret and sorrow on both sides, so deeply felt that both Raimondin and Melusine swoon for a time, the inevitable must happen. The faery must return whence she came, to the Otherworld, in whatever condition that may be, leaving her beloved husband and children behind. Passing through a window has an iconic symbolism in that she passes from one condition of existence to another.

This is no private occasion of grief and disaster. The whole countryside becomes witness to it as she flies over her beloved land, uttering cries of distress, in her dragon form. She even rocks the castle tower when she lands upon it, dislodging a stone. As it was she who built the structure in the first place, it would perhaps have been no surprise if the whole place had tumbled about the humans' head and ears.

There remain popular stories all around Poitou concerning buildings associated with her, that lose a stone each year, and which are difficult or impossible to replace. As we shall see, the theme also appears in the story of Geoffrey and his struggle with a phantom knight of the Poitevin tower.

22. Melusine's return.
This is an on going sequence which may not be finished yet.

The first occasion is a moving addendum to the story of Melusine, emphasising that despite all, she is at heart a loving mother whose first concern is the welfare of the youngest of her human family, returning to suckle Raymond and Thierry, who are still babes in arms.

The sighting of Melusine by the children's nurses is however the first of a whole series of visitations to announce the death of lords of the Lusignan line or a change of ownership of her castle. In this she fulfils the role of the traditional *bean sidhe*. And after all, is she not one worthy to be regarded as one of the Sidhe, the lordly ones of the hollow hills?

There are, moreover, reasons to think that Melusine is a presence and a power that remains, making her presence felt in various ways to the present day. In which case if you approach her romance in the right way, you may find yourself a witness at first hand! Who knows?

Chapter Four

✦

The Ten Sons of Melusine

N THE romance Melusine gave birth to ten sons, and possibly as a result of her faery origins, most of them were marked with features out of the ordinary.

Thus **Urien**, the oldest, although a fine figure of a man, had one eye higher than the other, one red and the other green, along with a very big mouth and huge ears, "as big as basket handles".

Eudes, the second, had one ear very big and the other very small.

Guy, the third, had one eye higher than the other but was otherwise very good looking.

Antoine, the fourth, had a birthmark upon his cheek like the paw of a lion, which by his eighth year had developed fur and claws.

Renaud, the fifth, had only one eye but with it could see for twenty leagues.

Geoffrey, the sixth, was nicknamed Great-tooth on account of one tooth, larger than a thumb, that projected from his mouth like the tusk of a boar.

Fromont, the seventh, had a little furry patch, like that of a mole or ferret, at the end of his nose.

Horrible, the eighth, had three eyes, one in the middle of his forehead.

Raymond, the ninth (also called Raymonnet), and **Thiérry**, the tenth, were babes in arms at the time of Mélusine's disappearance, and had no distinctive marks.

The fact that there are ten sons might to suggest to a Qabalistic student that the ten Sephiroth of the Tree of Life might be involved, but this does not seem to be the case. The character, appearance or function of the sons do not appear to correspond to any known esoteric system.

It has been suggested that the disfigurements indicate some trace of animality, as most are related to organs of sense – eyes, ears, nose, mouth. Although apart from Renaud's single eye, which can see for twenty leagues, there is no record of super-sensitivity of function as might be associated with a creature of the wild. Nor are any remarkable powers associated with Horrible's third eye.

Geoffrey's boar-like tusk is certainly consonant with his wild and boar like nature, for when provoked he would turn scarlet with rage and froth at the mouth. And there is of course a resonance with the magical boar that lured Raimondin and Count Aymeri into the forest. It is Geoffrey too whose story has most ancient mythopoeic elements within it, and which impinges most strongly on the fate of Raimondin and Melusine.

There may well be some symbolic significance in the lion paw mark on the cheek of Antoine. However, this is never explained, any more than in the romances of Chrétien de Troyes, where in *Yvain*, a hero marries a faery and forms an alliance with a lion, or in *Le Conte del Graal*, a lion's paw remains affixed to Gawain's shield in the Castle of Maidens – a faery establishment if ever there was one.

The tales of the elder sons are for the most part stories of adventure, and have no mythopoeic element. They serve the dynastic interests of the patrons who commissioned the romance, linking the faery line to Cyprus, Little Armenia, Luxembourg, Bohemia, and the county of La Marche.

Taking up a large part of the romance of Jean d'Arras, although Couldrette abbreviated them somewhat in his verse version, they remain informative documents on the techniques of 14th century warfare and in this capacity served as instructional manuals, as well as sources of inspiration, for many aspiring young knights. These elements are however of more interest to military historians than to esoteric students so we will not pursue them in any detail.

Our interest lies on the inner side of the romance – which is revealed in the story of Melusine and Raimondin, of Melusine's faery kin, and to some extent that of Geoffrey. The only thing ancient in the adventures of the elder sons – and some elements of Geoffrey's story – are fragments of garbled family history over the previous couple of hundred years.

Four of the elder sons divide into convenient pairs whose adventures fulfil the ambitions and wildest dreams of any landless knight of the time. That is, to find a rich heiress who is in distress, come to her rescue, marry her and become lord of her domain. This did indeed happen to a happy few in real life, some of whom were Lusignans, of which more later.

Thus **Urien** and **Guy** sail off to the East fighting Saracens, in the course of which they become rulers of Cyprus and of Little Armenia (a territory on the south coast of modern Turkey founded by emigrants from Greater Armenia around 1060 under pressure from nomadic invaders from the east.) Urien marries the princess Hermine of Cyprus, and Guy the princess Florie of Little Armenia. All four, it should be stressed, are fictional characters. There is however a vague historical background to some of this in that real life Lusignans did establish dynasties in Cyprus and Little Armenia in the 12th and 13th centuries, which lasted for some time.

The other pair of elder sons, **Antoine** and **Renaud**, also go off adventuring, in their case into the heartlands of Europe. In the course of this, Antoine picks up the Duchy of Luxembourg and the hand of its heiress Christine, while Renaud becomes King of Bohemia through marriage to the princess Eglantine. These are also all fictional characters, and their story serves to establish a semi-plausible link between the line of Lusignan and that of Luxembourg and Bohemia from which the Duke of Berry was descended. In the course of time as the Melusine story became more widely known a number of other families also tried to jump on the bandwagon by means of tampered genealogies and similarities – real or adjusted – of their coats of arms.

Whilst the facial disfigurements of the sons of Melusine are thought to be a consequence of their parentage, there is also much about their actions that pertain to the faery too.

Urien, Guy, Antoine and Renaud all have a natural desire to go off adventuring. With the first two this may take the form of crusading but, as with some of the historical crusaders, an important underlying motive was the acquisition of land and the founding of a dynasty. This is much in the spirit of the forest clearing, populating, building instincts of a medieval faery who has crossed the divide between the races to marry a human. Such was the case with the unnamed faery who married Raimondin's father, Hervé de Leon, and helped him establish the County of Forez. It is also the gist of the story of Melusine with Raimondin, and their sons are primarily builders of dynasties rather than holy warriors. Whilst Urien and Guy did most of their fighting against Saracens, in the case of Antoine and Renaud it was Slavs rather than Saracens they fought in Bohemia, whilst in Luxembourg they were up against fellow Christians.

Eudes was likewise one with dynastic ambitions although in a more peaceful way, staying closer to home and becoming, also through marriage but without need for conflict, the Count of La Marche. (There was however a great deal more trouble in historical fact, for the county became much disputed territory between the House of Anjou and the House of Lusignan.)

Whilst the stories of the older brothers were written largely to make dynastic points, that of **Geoffrey** contains mythopoeic elements plainly of ancient provenance. Nonetheless he does embark on a voyage to the east to join Uriens and Guy and the Grand Master of Rhodes in harassing the Saracens, and in particular the Sultan of Damascus, which is partly the garbled memory of an historical Geoffrey of Lusignan who was a hero of the 3rd Crusade.

On his return home Geoffrey goes off to Ireland where Raimondin's rule is threatened by insurrection. Needless to say there is no historical basis in the Lusignans ever having possessions in Ireland, which was more the provenance of their great enemy Henry Plantagenet. However, after some exciting skirmishes and lively guerrilla warfare, having hanged the rebel ring leaders, Geoffrey comes home again and begins to make a reputation as a giant killer.

Here we move from fictional history to genuine myth and legend, in the course of which he is destined to discover the tomb of his grandfather, Helias, lit by a perpetual light in a faery mountain, along with an account of the faery history of Melusine's family before she arrived in Poitou.

Geoffrey's boar-like behaviour and great rages may have helped him become a formidable killer of giants but on the debit side caused him to kill his brother and to hound his uncle, the Count of Forez, to death.

The brother he killed, **Fromont**, was the pious one of the family who sought a religious life at the abbey of Mervaille. This caused his father Raimondin some concern but Melusine welcomed it. However it provoked such ferocious rage in Geoffrey that he burned down the abbey, with Fromont and all the monks inside it.

This contains a certain degree of family memory in that there was an historical Geoffrey (the son of the famous crusader), something of a wild character, who set fire to the abbey of Maillezais some time in the 13th century, and had a record of conflict with the monks, although not to the point of mass murder.

However, Geoffrey of the romance is not an evil character, but more a tragic case of an excess of the natural, the instinctive, the wild. It is not a devious and self-serving violence of which he is capable. He reacts to situations spontaneously and with almost the innocence of the completely instinctive. In much the same way that a wild beast will pounce on its prey.

If any of the sons can be reckoned evil then it must be the grotesque **Horrible**, who was indeed something of a monster. A huge baby, he had three eyes, the third in the middle of his forehead, and a nature that matched his name. Apparently born with teeth, he caused the death of two wet-nurses by ferociously biting them, and did not survive beyond the age of four. He was put to death on Melusine's advice in view of the carnage he might wreak if allowed to grow to manhood. He was lured into a cave and asphyxiated by the smoke of a fire built at its mouth, but was accorded a fine funeral and magnificent tomb.

The two youngest sons, **Raymond** and **Thierry**, seem however to have been without physical defect, and were babes in arms when Melusine disappears. They demonstrate in the romance the tender motherly feelings of the banished faery as she secretly reappears, to the astonishment of the nurses, to suckle them both.

The importance of the two youngest children for the patrons of the romance was in light of current historical and dynastic claims. Thus Raymond is credited with becoming the Count of Forez and Thierry the Lord of Parthenay. The latter fact is considerably elaborated in Couldrette's rhymed version, commissioned by William l'Archeveque XII, Lord of Parthenay, which goes out of its way to emphasise that Thierry was nominated by Melusine to be the heir of Parthenay, and later, at the death of Geoffrey, also of Lusignan.

Jean d'Arras on the other hand, writing for the Duke of Berry, makes no mention of this.

The Duke of Berry's claims to the line of Lusignan were considerably more tenuous. He had been granted rulership of

Poitou by his father, King Jean le Bon, for Lusignan had been claimed by the French throne when the main family line died out in 1323. But after a crushing English victory at the Battle of Poitiers in 1356, King Jean was captured and taken off to the Tower of London, and the whole of Poitou ceded to England. This uneasy peace soon broke down and the whole countryside erupted into war again, and in 1373 the town of Lusignan was taken by the French, although the almost impregnable castle held out for another eighteen months.

In the end the Duke had more or less to bribe the English out to gain the castle – but not before Melusine had appeared to the English commander Creswell one night, as confirmation that the castle was about to change hands.

This remarkable account was made much of at the time, and sworn to by Creswell "through every possible oath a man of honour could take", albeit when a prisoner of the Duke. It was also taken as evidence that the faery approved of the change of ownership.

Creswell told how when he was lying in bed in the castle one night with his mistress, a woman called Alexandra, an enormous serpent appeared, with a tail seven or eight feet long, banded blue and silver, the Lusignan colours. He did not know how it could have entered for the doors were locked and there was a great fire burning in the hearth.

It began to beat its tail on the bed, although not hurting them, but when he sat up and seized his sword Alexandra said "Don't be frightened! It is only the lady of the fortress, who built it. She will do us no harm, but has come to tell you to surrender the place."

The serpent then changed into a tall and beautiful lady, wearing clothes of a bygone era, and sat by the fire, occasionally looking toward the bed so that Creswell could clearly see her face.

Then an hour before dawn she changed back into a serpent, again beating the floor with her tail and the bed round their feet, although still without hurting them, before she disappeared.

Jean d'Arras also cites a man named Godard who lived within the fortress and who claimed to have seen Melusine many times near a well. Particularly one where it was said, as late as the 16th century, that anyone who listened carefully could hear treasure being moved around in the depths below. Whilst Prince Yvain of

Wales (who was fighting on the French side) also swore that he saw Melusine twice on the walls of Lusignan three days before the fortress surrendered.

This was all in support of the Duke of Berry's desire to bolster his claim to the territory. As a great patron of the arts the idea of commissioning a romance, suggested by his sister Marie, Duchess of Bar, must have appealed to him, evoking local folklore on his side.

The rhymed version by Couldrette, which is somewhat shorter, cutting back on many of the adventures of the elder sons, was more sympathetic to the English, although by the time the romance had been completed, its original sponsor William Archeveque had died, and the family decided to throw in their lot with the French.

So the stories of Melusine's sons are for the most part fictional with a fair amount of mythopoeic material in the case of Geoffrey, which we will treat at length in the next chapter. Otherwise the other brothers as presented in the romance need not detain us. What history is contained in them is very tenuous and fragmentary but in search of those who might be regarded true "sons of Melusine", various lords and younger sons of the Lusignan line, we shall devote a chapter to an account of various crusaders, courtly lovers and kings who form part of the historical record of the human kin of Melusine.

Chapter Five

❧

Geoffrey the Giant Killer

N CONTRAST to the accounts of the other sons of Melusine, that of Geoffroy la Grand'Dent or Geoffrey Great-Tooth is full of mythopoeic material. It occurs in different episodes, which cover his role as a giant killer, first close to home, and then in Northumberland, where he enters a magic mountain to find the tomb of Melusine's father and an account of his faery ancestry; and finally in a contest with a strange visitant in the Poitevin Tower at Lusignan. Also on the mundane plane is an event that impacts mightily on the main story – the murder of his brother Fromont – provoking the break-up of the marriage of Raimondin and Melusine.

We need not follow his fighting in Ireland or in Palestine against the Sultan of Damascus. These are entirely secular affrays, and there is probably more than enough blood and guts to suit most readers in the accounts of his single combat with otherworldly creatures.

We will however take brief account of his final relationship to his father Raimondin and his younger brothers Raymond and Thierry, and glance at the historical record of his prototype in two Geoffreys of the Lusignan line.

Geoffrey and the giant Guédon of Guerandais
In the district of Guerandais the giant Guédon had been extracting tribute from the people for some time but it seemed to be beyond the powers of Raimondin to deal with him. Indeed Raimondin was much concerned to prevent Geoffrey from finding out about it, for fear that he would insist on going to fight the giant, who was reckoned to be invincible.

"What the devil?" cried Geoffrey, when he found out, "I come back from exacting tribute from the Sultan of Damascus, and then hang the rebels in Ireland, only to find this stinking dog raising taxes on our land?"

He forthwith took up arms and left with nine companions for the Guerandais and the mountain where the giant lived. He ordered his men to stay behind and went alone up a great flight of stairs cut into the rock. Outside the castle at the top he stood at the drawbridge and shouted:

"Where is the traitor making war on my country? Come on out and be killed!"

The giant put his head, the size of a bull, over the battlements, and when he saw Geoffrey Great Tooth all alone, rushed out swearing that it was an insult for just one man to seek to fight him. He stood more than fifteen feet tall and was armed with battle scythe, an iron whip, and three throwing hammers tucked into his belt.

Geoffrey fearlessly advanced toward him.

"Who are you?" demanded the astonished giant.

"They call me Geoffrey Great-Tooth, and I've come to cut off your head!"

"And you think you can do it?" sneered Guédon. "I could smash you to pulp with a single blow. But I will give you a chance and let you go, in pity for being so young and stupid."

"You are the stupid one," cried Geoffrey, "so pity yourself while you can!" And he spurred forward with all the strength of his horse and knocked the giant over backwards with a blow of his lance to the chest.

The giant leaped to his feet, furious at having been struck to the ground by a single blow.

"That was a fine present you brought me," he snarled, "so it is only right that I give you one back!" And he swung his scythe and cut the legs of Geoffrey's horse from under him.

Geoffrey leaped clear of the stricken horse and drew his sword. Throwing himself into the fray, he struck the giant such a blow on the arm that the scythe fell useless from his hands. Then he followed up by wounding him in the hip. Guédon struck back with his iron whip at Geoffrey's helm and almost felled him, but he gave the giant such a blow with his mace that it made him drop the whip. Guédon now siezed a hammer from his belt and threw it with all his force, striking Geoffrey's mace from his hand.

The giant leaped forward to seize the fallen mace but Geoffrey struck him such a blow with his sword that he severed his arm at the elbow. Arm and mace fell to the ground, and the giant, maddened with pain, took a flying kick at Geoffrey. Geoffrey dodged and with another prodigious blow cut the giant's leg in two as well.

The giant fell, imploring his gods to come to his aid, but Geoffrey finished him off with a final blow that cleaved his helm and his head down to the teeth. Then he cut off Guédon's head, took up his horn and sounded it three times. His men came running to find him standing over the body of the vanquished giant.

Comment

This is fairly straightforward action-comic stuff that has been a staple of entertainment at one level or another throughout cultural history. However, in the context of the times it also indicates a principle of the sanctity of land ownership – for in Geoffrey's eyes the giant's main offence is exacting taxes to which he has no right. Any burden of tax upon the populace should after all go into the coffers of the Lusignans.

On a more mythopoeic level we often find in giant stories a personification of ancient titanic forces that ruled the earth before the advent of humankind, and which still wreak havoc in natural disasters of earthquake, volcano, flood, storm, drought, pestilence, climate change. All of which are less easily dealt with than by hiring a giant killer. In this respect Geoffrey represents a hero figure of what humanity aspires to be able to do. There is however an element of savagery in Geoffrey, insofar that he plays the giants at their own game, which is out and out physical violence.

This, however, can have a disastrous effect if employed in the human world, as occurs when Geoffrey returns from killing the giant.

Geoffrey and Fromont and the monks of Maillezais abbey

While Geoffrey was fighting the giant, his younger brother Fromont sought an audience with Raimondin. He was a young man of great grace and wisdom, and spent much of his time at the abbey of Maillezais where he went to pray. Now he sought his father's permission to take up the religious life.

Raymondin was astonished. "Why become a monk?" he said. "Look at your elder brothers who are all noble knights. Become a monk? No, that's impossible! Why become a priest when you can be a knight?"

But Fromont replied: "I do not want to become a knight, or to carry arms. I would rather pray to God, for you, for my mother and all my brothers. Let me be a monk in the abbey of Maillezais. It is my greatest wish. I love the place and want to spend my life there, so please do not refuse me."

Raymondin saw that despite his own misgivings, Fromont's mind was made up, so he sent a messenger to see what Melusine might think. She was building a fortress at Niort, whose fine twin towers can still be seen. In reply to Raimondin she said: "It is for Fromont to choose. I submit to his will. His decision will be mine."

On learning this Raimondin called his son to him.

"Fromont," he said, "your mother has given her consent but I beg you to think a little more. The monks of Maillezais that you wish to join are said to be crude, unmannerly, rough, and coarse. So why not choose a better monastery? What about Marmoutier? That is a splendid place! Or, if you wish, Bourg-Dieu. But then, why be just a monk? Why not become a canon? You could be a canon at Poitiers and have a situation that is three times better – and maybe go on to the great church of St Martin at Tours. I could even settle and sign the charters for Notre Dame at Chartres if you wish. Or what about Notre Dame at Paris, for I know the Pope! Nothing is impossible for me! Eventually you could be a bishop! Of Paris, Arras or Beauvais! So say, Fromont, wouldn't you rather be a canon?"

"No," said Fromont, "I want to be a monk – and at Maillezais. That is the place I have chosen and would wish for no other for the rest of my life."

"In the name of God," Raymondin said, "if that is your wish, then go, and pray to God for us there."

"I will not fail to do so," said Fromont, "if it is God's will."

Thereupon he dressed in the Benedictine habit and the monks of Maillezais joyfully welcomed him.

Geoffrey was still in Guérandais, fêted by all the country for killing the giant. Messengers now came from far away Northumberland to ask for his services there, where a cruel and dangerous giant was devastating the land. Geoffrey had no wish to leave the country of his birth, but felt it his duty to go to their aid.

As he was preparing to leave, another message came, this time from Raimondin, telling him Fromont had become a monk.

The thought filled Geoffrey with rage. His face suffused with blood and he foamed at the mouth like a boar, whilst all around him trembled in fear.

"What? Haven't my father and mother enough wealth to provide for my brother? To give him land and castles and marry richly instead of becoming a monk? God's teeth, those debauched and treacherous monks must have bewitched my brother and lured him to their house to gain some honour for themselves. I know he used to spend days and nights with them, and by God that never pleased me! But they will rue the day they persuaded him to join them."

He told the messengers from Northumberland to await his return, and set off for Maillezais. The monks were meeting in the chapter house when he arrived, the abbot reading an epistle to them. When they learned of Geoffrey's arrival they went out to meet him, rejoicing at his visit, but Geoffrey, enflamed with rage, addressed them brutally.

"What gave you debauched monks the audacity to bewitch my brother with your fawning hypocrisies? To become a monk in this place and give up knighthood? God's teeth, you made a great mistake there, and now will drink a bitter cup!"

He ground his teeth and frowned so horribly that even his henchmen were afraid and some monks wept with fright. But the abbot replied, "Sir, the decision was his own, not mine, and I believe it to be sincere. It was his piety that caused him to enter our order, and that is the truth. Here is your brother! Ask him yourself!"

"Brother," said Fromont, "in truth I swear to you, no one persuaded me to become a monk. I acted of my own accord, and now I am a monk, a monk I shall remain. Our father and mother approved my wish, and I pray God, dear brother, that you do so too."

"On my head," said Geoffrey, almost mad with rage, "then you will pay for it too! No one will ever taunt me with having a monk for a brother!"

Enflamed with grief and fury he ran out, barricading the doors behind him. Then he sent for bales of straw and had them piled against the building, swearing to set light to them.

His knights approached to reason with him, saying that Fromont had told the truth, and by the sanctity of his life and his prayers he could bring great help to the souls of his relatives and friends.

"God's teeth," shouted Geoffrey, "neither he nor any other monk in there will sing mass or matins again. I am going to burn the lot of them!"

The knights now retreated saying they wanted no part in this crime.

Geoffrey seized one of the lamps from the church and set fire to the straw. At first nothing could be seen but smoke, but soon the fire took hold and engulfed the chapter house, entrapping all the monks inside. That day the abbot and a hundred monks were burned, along with Fromont, and the greater part of the abbey.

Then seeing what he had done Geoffrey was filled with remorse, tormented by the death of his brother, the abbot and all the other monks, and the ruin of the beautiful abbey. Sorrowing and in despair at the crime he had committed, he took leave of no one, but set sail for Northumberland with ten of his men, not caring if death should wait him there.

Comment

This is a tragic story and one that reveals the dual side of Geoffrey as well as giving an insight into secular views of the church. Both Raimondin and Geoffrey see things from a mundane point of view, and largely in terms of wealth and power. Raimondin trying to tempt Fromont to worldly success by political ambition within the ecclesiastical hierarchy has its amusing side, but reveals an attitude that was perhaps as rife within the church as without it. It was this kind of thing within a medieval church that sought to be a secular power itself that brought about the Reformation and all that stemmed from it.

Neither Raimondin nor Geoffrey have many illusions about the piety of the monks themselves, either, although this may be to some extent a layman's prejudice. Thinking the worst of what they do not understand is much the same attitude as that taken by Raimondin's brother, the Count of Forez, who suspected the worst of Melusine – again "supported" by popular rumour on no evidence whatever. And this, when finally accepted by Raimondin himself, provoked by Geoffrey's actions, spells ultimate disaster.

We see Geoffrey, as Raimondin doubtless saw him, in the grip of a demonic force of spite and revenge. This may have had its value in more primitive times of tribal conflict and blood feud but it has no place in a civilised society. In one respect the constant irruption of war in human history could be seen as a primitive giant working from the depths of humanity itself, in which case Geoffrey is hardly a giant killer, but rather, a puppet of the giants themselves.

To Raimondin's ultimate disaster he identifies this demonic or instinctive ferocity with the fount of faeryland itself. Melusine, however, comes out of this situation with wisdom and compassion; not that it saves her in face of Raimondin's all too human reaction.

Geoffrey and the giant Grimaut at the magic mountain in Northumberland

As soon as Geoffrey landed in Northumberland, the local people gathered round to tell how the ferocious giant had been known to kill a hundred knights in a single day, as well as over a thousand ordinary people, and that no known person could stand up to him.

"He sounds like a devil, a veritable demon, but if I find him he will perish at my hands. Give me a guide to show me where he lives. You will not see me again until I have killed him."

They gave him a guide and recommended them both to God as they rode off toward a high mountain. As they approached they could see the giant, sat under a tree beside a block of marble.

The guide, sweating and white faced, trembled at the sight. "Almighty God," he cried, "I would not go near that mountain for all the money in the world."

Geoffrey laughed and invited him to stay to watch the fight.

But the guide replied, "I am not staying here. I have guided you faithfully. I just want to go now."

Geoffrey laughed again and said, "You have no need to join in! You only need stay until you have seen who wins. Then you can join your friends and tell them of my fate."

"I will do as you say, sir," replied the guide, "but if you knew that devil Grimaut as well as I do, you wouldn't take another step!"

"I'm not afraid!" replied Geoffrey, "He will not stand against me!"

So saying, he left the guide in the plain and started up the mountain.

Grimaud marvelled to see a single man coming on his own. He said to himself, "He must be coming to sue for peace. I will go and hear what he says."

He took up a great staff that would have been too heavy for any mere human to lift, but to him was as light as a child finds a stick.

He waited for Geoffrey to approach and cried, "Well? Who are you, and what do you want? Don't say you come to challenge me? For if so, you will surely die!"

"Bandit," retorted Geoffrey, "I defy you to try and kill me! I will cut off your head first, and see what you can do then!"

Grimaut burst out laughing. "Oh, spare my life, good sir, I beg you! Let me off and ransom me!"

"Poor fool," said Geoffrey, "do you think to mock me? I would not dream of a ransom. I would rather split your skull down to the teeth!"

Then Geoffrey put his shield before him, spurred his horse, and with all his might struck the giant full in the chest with his lance, piercing the steel chain mail and wounding Grimaut piteously. The giant fell to the ground, his legs in the air, struggling to regain his feet as Geoffrey dismounted and looked down at him.

"Just who are you?" the giant demanded. "I have never taken a blow like that before, or ever been knocked down. Before I take revenge, tell me where you are from. Are you secretly a famous knight?"

"I do not seek to hide my name," replied Geoffrey. "They call me Geoffrey Great-Tooth, and I am a son of Melusine, the noble lady of Lusignan."

"I know you well," said the giant, "and have heard tell of you. You killed my cousin Guédon in Guérandais. Well now you will get your reward, for I will avenge him!"

"So do they prattle on, who think they tell the truth," said Geoffrey. "You need more than puffed up pride to take revenge! I have met your type before!"

Before such mockery the giant could not contain himself. He aimed a blow at Geoffrey but his great staff missed and gouged a hole in the ground a foot deep. Geoffrey struck at the giant's arm with his sword and broke through the chain mail above the elbow. The blood flowed to the ground and stained the grass red.

The giant recovered and came on at Geoffrey once more, but missed again. This time the end of his staff buried itself three feet in the ground and broke in two.

With all his strength Geoffrey struck with his sword at the giant's head. The giant tottered, although he was not wounded, and returned a blow with his fist to Geoffrey's helm. Geoffrey was stunned but the blow broke a bone in the giant's hand, causing the fist to swell. Now Geoffrey redoubled the onslaught with his sword, and cut through the mail at the shoulder of the giant and into the flesh beneath. The giant's blood ran down his chest so that he was red to the feet. Grimaut cursed his gods, and threatened to deny them if they did not come to his aid.

He threw himself at Geoffrey and locked his arms around him to crush him to death. Geoffrey, fighting for breath, pummelled at his flanks, then reached for the knife that the giant wore at his belt. Drawing it, he stabbed again and again with it, piercing the chain mail hauberk, and causing the blood to flow. Forced to let go, the giant jumped back, now greatly afraid. He ran off up the mountain and disappeared in a cleft in the rock.

Distraught at having lost the giant, Geoffrey went back to his horse and returned to his guide, who marvelled at his courage when he saw how his helm was battered and the mail of his hauberk broken in places throughout.

A crowd of people gathered and hearing that the giant had run away, one of the barons asked if Geoffrey had told him his name. When he said that he had, the baron replied, "Then for all the gold in the world he will never come near you again. He knows he will not leave your hands alive. For his destined fate is to die at the hands of a descendent of Lusignan.

"The mountain in which he is hiding is the domain of faeries. King Helinas of Albany was imprisoned here by three of his daughters, for having broken faith with their mother Pressine. No one knows where the three girls went but Helinas never left here. And ever since there has been a giant to guard his marvellous cave. Grimaut is the fifth or sixth giant who has lived here, winter and summer, devastating the country until you came."

Geoffrey rejoiced to hear this news and swore he would not leave until he had found the giant again. He returned to the cleft in the rock where Grimaut had entered the mountain.

Looking within he could see nothing but a deep crevice.

"I cannot understand," said Geoffrey, "how a giant as big as he is passed through here. But if he entered then so can I, and whatever the cost, nothing will stop me. He may have disappeared into the earth, but I will go there too. And if he is there, I will find him!"

He slid his lance before him into the hole and followed after, feet first, as both he and the lance hurtled down the steep slope of a shaft to the bottom. Coming to himself he took up his lance, and holding it before him, felt his way through the darkness. After a while he began to see light some distance before him. It came from a magnificent chamber, cut into the solid rock, that opened out on all sides.

It was of marvellous beauty, covered with beaten gold and decorated with gems. In the middle was a rich tomb, supported by six massive golden pillars, embedded with precious stones from the mountain. Lying upon it was the chalcedony effigy of an armed king, at whose feet was the statue of a noble lady, holding a tablet upon which these words were carved.

> *Here lies the noble King Helinas, who lost me through his fault and to his misfortune.*
>
> *This noble king was my husband, who swore to me before we married never when I was giving birth would he ask where I was or seek to see me. Now it came about that from one conception I gave birth to three gracious and clever daughters.*
>
> *Now Helinas betrayed his oath looking in upon my bed, at which I departed from him nobody knew where, and took my daughters with me, to Avalon in fairyland. There I nourished them with my own milk, and they grew more and more beautiful.*
>
> *When they were fifteen years old I told them how their father lost me and how I fled with them to Avalon. The one called Melusine convinced her sisters that I sought vengeance on their father. They agreed to cast a spell on him and enclosed him in a mountain.*

When he died I had this tomb made with his effigy upon it so that whoever read this tablet could recall him to memory. I assigned a giant to stand guard from that hour so none would enter here if not descended from our line.

I decreed that on every Saturday Melusine would take on serpent form, and if she ever married her husband must never approach her on that day, or if he should see her in that state never speak of it to anyone. She could then live and die as a natural mortal woman.

Melior I banished to a castle in Armenia where she would keep a hawk. If any knight of high station succeed in standing watch over it for three nights without sleep, then he could have whatever gift he desired, apart from Melior herself. But if they fell asleep or dozed in any way they would remain forever as a prisoner.

Palastine I set to guard the treasure of her father in the high mountain of Canagou in Aragon, until such time as a knight of our lineage should by his own prowess climb to the top and win the treasure, with which to conquer the Promised Land.

I am Pressine, mother of the three daughters who were so clever and beautiful and upon whom I took this vengeance for having imprisoned their father Hellinas the king in the mountain in Avalon. For I loved him deeply however much he may have wronged me.

Geoffrey marvelled at reading this, not yet realising that he himself was of that lineage. Then he started to look for Grimaud.

He left the chamber and pressed on until, on the other side of a wall, he found himself in a beautiful field in the centre of which stood a square tower, big, powerful and well fortified. Seeing the door was open he went inside, brandishing his lance. Here he found many prisoners confined in a great cage. They were astonished to see him and warned him to hide before the giant returned if he valued his life. Geoffrey smiled, his great lance poised, and said he intended to fight.

At this point the giant arrived and seeing Geoffrey Great-Tooth realised that his end had come. He rushed into another room, slamming the door behind him. Geoffrey furiously belaboured the door until, with a kick, he knocked it from its hinges, despite the bolts. The giant, who was armed with a great square hammer, struck at Geoffrey's head, leaving him stunned, and without his solid helm he would have been killed.

Geoffrey staggered and said, "That was a good blow, but I've brought a better one for you!"

He drew his sword and thrust it up to the hilt in the giant's chest, who with a great cry crashed to the ground stone dead. Geoffrey wiped his sword and returned it to its sheath. Then he turned to the prisoners, of whom there were more than two hundred, and asked why they were imprisoned. They told him it was because of the tribute owed to the giant that they had not been able to pay. Geoffrey said, "Then rejoice, for you are released from all that. I came here so that he might no longer do you wrong. I have now killed him and paid your tribute for you!"

All rejoiced and begged Geoffrey to release them. He searched around, found the keys, opened the cage of their prison and gave them leave to go. They blessed the hour that Geoffrey came to deliver them and asked him to become their lord, for their king was dead. But Geoffrey declined to stay, for he wanted to return to Lusignan, and see his mother and father again.

He made haste to depart and rode at a great gallop to the sea with his men and embarked on a ship. In full sail before a favourable wind, it was evening as they approached Guérande, and everyone came to meet him, men, women and little children to make him great welcome, along with the great barons.

Comment

This is an account very rich in mythic elements. Not least the journey into the Earth in order to discover secrets of the ancestors. This is no mere archaeological dig, for as the old spiritual alchemical rubric has it, "visit the interior of the Earth to find the hidden stone".

As R.J. Stewart has amply demonstrated in *The UnderWorld Initiation* and elsewhere, this is an area of rich exploration, and not at all the root of all evil as previous authorities might have had us believe. Here it is a place of revelation for Geoffrey to discover the faery origins of his lineage, and whilst the giant may have his inner lair and keep his prisoners within these regions, it is the place where he can finally be defeated. The image of the hidden sepulchre, glowing with precious stones and lit with perpetually burning lights, in which is the body of a king, is a very powerful dynamic in western mystery tradition, and here we see presented, at the end of the 14th century, what was to become powerful Rosicrucian imagery at the beginning of the 17th century.

The mountain in which all this takes place I have called a magic mountain. It is in Northumberland, but seems to have an ambivalent existence, being located in Avalon too! It is thus, we might say, an otherworldly overlay (or underlay) of a natural physical feature as is recognised in many sacred places, although it is also a universal phenomenon did we but realise it. It is just that at some places the veil is thinner than at others. My personal preference for a location is at or around Bamborough Head, which is indeed a magical place to visit, and its castle associated with Sir Lancelot's Joyous Garde.

The message held by the statue of Pressine is a brief summary of essentials. In the romance this is a repetition of what has already been described at some length earlier on. We will reserve comment on this until our study of the kin of Melusine. It raises complex issues about Melusine's origins and why she should have her serpent tail. The story of a mother's curse upon three daughters is perhaps not to be taken too literally, and seems a later gloss on ancient material that romancers of the time did not fully understand.

Geoffrey's revenge on the Count of Forez

Geoffrey's young brother Raymond came to meet him on his return from Northumberland, embraced him tenderly, and took him to a room apart. Here he broke the news to him how they had lost their mother, Melusine.

Geoffrey trembled with grief and rage when he realised how he had provoked his father's wrath by burning Fromont to death. Then he remembered the tablet he had read in the mountain of Avalon on the tomb of King Helinas, and realised that Melusine was the daughter of that king and that King Helinas was his ancestor along with the faery Pressine. Then the thought came to him how Raimondin, his father, had first been pushed to betray Melusine. It was through the words of his brother, the Count of Forez. Thereupon Geoffrey swore to kill him.

With his brother and ten knights, Geoffrey left for Forez but so eager and well horsed was he, that he arrived in the county before them. The Count was in the great hall with his council as Geoffrey marched in and stood before them.

Like a man who has lost his reason, he drew his sword and cried, "Traitor! Prepare to die! It was you who lost me my mother!"

The Count's blood froze, knowing full well the cause of Geoffrey's rage. He turned and fled, frightened for his life. He ran madly to the tower of the keep and rushed up the stairs two by two, with Geoffrey close behind, followed by all the Count's men, seeking to save their master and beseeching Geoffrey to spare his life.

But Geoffrey kept at the heels of the Count, swearing he would do him to death for the loss of his mother. The Count climbed to the top of the keep, where, as he could flee no farther, he jumped through a window onto a sloping roof. Here his foot slipped, he slid down the tiles, and plunged to his death on the rocks below.

After this miserable and shameful death Geoffrey remained for the funeral and then announced to the barons that from now on they would have his brother Raymond for their lord, as the new Count of Forez.

Comment

We include this for completeness of Geoffrey's tale. It throws little further light upon him that we did not know already. It is the beginning, however, of a more benign aspect of him as he sees to the welfare of his younger brother Raymond, and at the same time rather subtly returns a more direct faery connection to the rulership of Forez, which had after all been founded by Geoffrey and Raymond's grandfather Hervé de Leon with the assistance of a mysterious faery partner who then disappeared, although with or without the same tragic circumstances as Melusine we do not know.

Geoffrey and his father Raimondin

Geoffroy now returned to Lusignan where his father remained lamenting, and suffered the more at learning of the death of his brother.

"I have more than enough to weep over," said Raimondin. "I have lost my wife, now I see my lineage disappearing through my fault and my sin. May Jesus Christ save my soul!"

Geoffrey begged his father's forgiveness for the crimes he had done. Raimondin, his eyes full of tears, said, "Forget the past! Nothing can restore your mother or your brother, no matter what we do. We can only pay honour to the dead. Rebuild the abbey and the fine buildings you destroyed when you burned the hundred monks in your anger, madness and outrageous pride."

"I will rebuild it," said Geoffrey, "if it please God, more beautiful than ever it was before."

"May you be judged by the result of your work," said Raimondin, "and I leave you to it. I am going on pilgrimage far away. I shall confess my sins to the holy apostle of Rome, Pope Leo, and then retire from this world. I leave you my country to guard, you and no other. Look after Thierry your young brother. I leave to him Parthenay – and the noble castles of Vouvant, Chastel-Aiglon and Meurvent will recognise his authority as far as La Rochelle. That was the wish of my beautiful Melusine before she departed – she had long spoken of it."

"I respect her wishes," said Geoffrey, "and will look after my brother Thierry, as you have asked me to do."

Raimondin prepared for his journey. All sighed to see their lord make his farewells and depart. Geoffrey and Thierry accompanied him for a part of the way, and then Geoffrey returned to Lusignan and Thierry to Parthenay.

Geoffrey restored the abbey of Maillezais to be more beautiful than it had ever been. Some mocked who heard of this, saying "Where does his holiness come from? Has Renard become a monk?" – in allusion to the story of Renard the fox who often claimed to be converted the better to pull off his tricks!

When Raimondin arrived in Rome he confessed his sins to the Holy Father, who marvelled at the prodigies he heard about Melusine, and then he left for Aragon to become a hermit at Montserrat, where in a cell halfway up this wild mountain he lived a long and devoted life. After his death, Geoffrey went down to Montserrat and built a tomb for him there, bestowing many gifts on the abbey.

Comment

This is a brief summing up of the eventual fate of Raimondin, and although he seems to have been at peace with himself and with holy church, there is a final twist in the story. This provides a reason for Geoffrey's conflict with a strange visitant at one of the towers of the castle at Lusignan, although there are some inconsistencies that point to a somewhat hasty bodging up of disparate elements by the romancers. Apart from this, the story points up the link between the domain of Parthenay and the Melusine line, through the youngest son, Thierry – an element that is particularly emphasised in the version by Couldrette, which was commissioned by the contemporary lords of Parthenay.

Geoffrey and the Phantom Knight of the Tower

For ten years after his father's death Geoffrey governed Lusignan without much care about being rendered accounts, until one day his servants persuaded him that this was something that he ought to do. He reluctantly consented to this and as a result was puzzled by an entry that had appeared for ten years past:

"Item: 10 sous for the pommel on the tower."

He asked what there was about the tower that cost ten sous for the pommel each year.

"Can't you build strong enough for something to last ten or twenty years without needing repair every year?"

"Oh no sir," they replied, "it is not for repairs, it is a tribute."

"What?" cried Geoffrey, "my only overlord for the land of Lusignan and its fortress is God, my creator! And along with him, I would like to be quit of this ten sous a year. To whom do you pay it?"

"In faith, sir, we do not know!"

"And you expect me to sign off the accounts?" said Geoffrey. "I want to see the receipts of whoever it is you claim to pay ten sous a year to for the pommel on my tower. God's teeth, he will not get it next time. He must reveal who he is and the reason I owe him anything. Otherwise either you or he will repay me all payments in the past."

His servants replied, "Sir, five or six years after your mother left your father, every year on the last day of August a great hand appeared which took the pommel that adorned the summit of the Poitevin tower and broke it – so savagely that it also brought down part of the roof. It required twenty or thirty pounds to repair it each year.

"Then a man came that your father had never seen, he said,

and advised him to put thirty silver pieces worth ten sous into a purse and have it left at the highest stage of the tower. These ten sous were put in a deerskin bag on the piece of wood that supports the pillar on which the ornamental ball is fixed. Every year after the pommel remained intact. We have done it ever since and the pommel has never been moved or damaged, although the next day the purse was gone."

Geoffrey reflected on these words for some time and then left the room in a fury. "Do not dare to pay any more," he shouted, "or it will be the worse for you. I will go and see who has the audacity to levy tribute for my own possessions. The day I accept anything like that may I die an atrocious death! Bring me the purse of silver the day you usually pay it."

Geoffrey also told his brothers about this – Thierry in Parthenay, Raymond in Forez, and Eudes in La Marche. When the last day of August arrived he heard mass and went to confession and made his communion with great fervour before going to where his brothers and the barons of the realm were at table. After the meal he armed himself head to toe and asked for the stole that the chaplain had worn that morning at mass. He put it round his neck and crossed it on his chest. Then he took the purse with thirty pieces of silver worth ten sous and hung that also round his neck, buckled on his sword, took his shield, and asked the chaplain to bless him with holy water. Finally he said to his brothers, "I commend you all to God. I am going to see if I can find whoever levies a tribute from the fortress of Lusignan. And if I am stronger than he and beat him then the silver will stay with me!"

Then he climbed to the highest part of the tower. His brothers and other lords stayed below, in great concern, for fear that he would be killed. But Geoffrey, afraid of nothing, waited high above to see what might come. There he stayed for most of the afternoon without seeing anything, until finally, a little after the hour of vespers he heard a great tumult and the roof of the tower began to tremble. Soon after, a great knight in armour appeared before him, who said, "What Geoffrey, do you think to deny me the rent received for the pommel of this tower? It is my due, and has been granted to me since your father's day!"

"Where are the deeds that refer to the matter?" demanded Geoffrey. "Show me why my father accepted this demand, and if

I see you have a right to that ball, then your money is ready for you here."

The other replied, "There are no deeds, but I have always been paid until now."

"My faith!" said Geoffrey. "You must take me for a fool to think to impose a duty on me without proving you have any right. Say then, who are you, to have levied a tax on my goods for fourteen or fifteen years? In the name of God Almighty I defy you! And demand back all you have been paid."

"My faith!" said the other. "You must fear nothing! For I am a creature of God and you will know my name in due time!"

Then without another word they started to fight, with ferocity and great blows, the noise of which could be heard by those at the foot of the tower.

When the knight realised how well Geoffrey fought with his sword he returned his own to its scabbard and threw his shield to the ground. Seeing this, Geoffrey threw down his own shield, and raising his sword in both hands, struck the knight on the helm so hard as to make him stagger. He followed up, caught hold of him and gave him another great blow with the pommel. The other gripped him with both arms and Geoffrey, dropping his sword, seized him in turn.

Now began a violent struggle as they struck each other with such force that they were bathed in sweat. The knight, seeing the purse, grabbed it by its cords to drag it from Geoffrey's neck, who seized it in his fist with the money still inside. The other pulled with all his strength until the cords broke, but Geoffrey kept the purse and money in his hand.

They had already fought so long that the sun had set.

Then Geoffrey took up his sword again in his right hand and cried "You have neither purse nor money yet, and it will cost you much blood if you do. But I'm amazed that you have fought so long."

"My faith," said the knight, "and I am even more astonished that you have been able to resist my strength. We will meet again tomorrow, for now it is getting too late. You will find me in the meadow on the other side of the river, mounted and armed, to claim my rights against you. But promise me that no one but yourself will cross."

"Very well," said Geoffrey, "I promise."

The other then disappeared and Geoffrey did not see how he went. "Oh well," he said, "that was an agile messenger. I wonder who he can be."

He went back down the stairs carrying the knight's shield that he had won. His brothers and the other lords asked him what had been happening. Geoffrey replied he had met a valiant knight who had done more harm to him than anyone else he had ever fought. And he told them all that had happened up to the sudden disappearance of the knight. Some began to laugh thinking it all a jest, saying that they had never heard such a tale before. But then seeing how Geoffrey's helmet was dented with blows and his armour broken they realised he was not joking. Geoffrey then disarmed and they went to dinner.

Very early next morning Geoffrey and his brothers rose and heard mass. Geoffrey took the bread dipped in the wine and armed himself, mounted his strong and fast horse, took up his shield and grasped his lance. His brothers and the barons accompanied him as far as the stream beside the meadow that lies on one side of Poitiers. There Geoffrey took leave of them and crossed.

There he found the knight armed at all points, shield at the ready, lance couched, mounted on a great grey horse. He had the air of a man full of vigour who showed no fear of any adversary.

When he saw the knight Geoffrey cried out, "Sir knight, are you the one who wants to levy a tax on my fortress?"

"Yes, indeed I am," replied the other.

"On your head be it." said Geoffrey. "I come to dispute your claim. Defend yourself!"

And they battled so hard that neither had shield or coat of mail that was not broken into a hundred pieces. They fought on until the end of the afternoon without either being the victor.

Finally the knight said, "Geoffrey, listen to me. I have tested you enough. As for your ten sous, you can keep them. But know that what I have done was for the good of your father's soul. The Pope gave him a penance to perform for breaking his oath to your mother, but he did not complete it. But now, if you agree to build a hospital and chapel for the health of your father's soul, your tower will remain in peace. Although it will continue to be a place where wonders occur more than anywhere else in the castle."

Geoffrey replied that he would willing do all this if he knew he was dealing with a being of God. The other swore that that was what he was.

"Then be sure I will do it," said Geoffrey, "but tell me who you are."

"Geoffrey, do not ask me more," replied the other, "for all you need to know is that I am a messenger from God."

Then he disappeared.

All returned to Lusignan where Geoffrey hung his armour in the great hall and from one of the pillars, they hung the shield he had taken from the knight. There it remained until Geoffrey had built the hospital and the chapel, when it disappeared and nobody knew where.

Comment

There are some inconsistencies in detail of this story, insofar that earlier Raimondin had been said to have left Lusignan almost immediately after the disappearance of Melusine, whereas here it appears that he continued to rule there for some five or six years.

There is also some confusion of place as well as time. The conflict takes place in the Poitevin tower at Lusignan, although the field where it is continued, apparently close by, turns out to be in Poitiers.

However, these are minor points that did not bother medieval writers too much, it seems, although they suggest that the story was added on to the main romance, almost as an afterthought.

Geoffrey was obviously a character who caught the imagination and indeed a completely separate romance cycle did later develop around him. The purpose of its inclusion in the Melusine story would seem to be to take account of a tradition directly associated with Melusine. Certain buildings associated with her in popular tradition were destined never to be completed. Some ornament or stone would be constantly thrown to the ground almost as some kind of poltergeist activity.

The church at Parthenay is one of these places, where the story goes that when Melusine built it one night, dawn came upon her unexpectedly and she did not have time to put in place the last stone at one of the windows. She left at great speed on horseback, the horse leaving the imprint of its shoe on the sill, but ever since then, masons have never succeeded in putting another stone in place.

A similar story is associated with a group of five other buildings, but originates at the castle of Pouzauges, an 11ᵗʰ century structure with twelve towers remarkably well preserved to this day. Melusine is said to have built it in three nights, much to the curiosity of the locals who saw the walls appear higher each morning. So a mason decided to keep watch one night, and at midnight by light of the moon he saw the faery carrying cement and stones in her apron. However, she realised she was being spied on and flew off, crying "Pouzauges, Tiffauges, Mervent, Châteaumur and Vouvant, will, I swear, lose a stone each year!" And ever since at these places the stones fall.

We have in all of this a confusion of the pure Melusine story with ancient goddess lore associated with superstitious belief about the origin of ancient stonework, be it prehistoric, Roman or early medieval. Any prominent female legendary figure is likely to be caught up in this, even Christian as with St. Radegonde who built an abbey at Poitiers, although it was Eleanor of Aquitaine and her kin who were responsible for much of the 12ᵗʰ century work. Which brings us naturally to consider the historical Geoffrey of Lusignan.

The historical Geoffrey
There are two historical Geoffreys of Lusignan, father and son, whose lives contribute at least in some small part to Geoffroy la Grand Dent of the romance. Neither of them is recorded to have had a great boar-like tooth, but they matched him in bravery in combat and even ferocity.

The elder Geoffrey was the elder brother of two more famous siblings, Amalric and Guy, whose remarkable lives we shall consider later. He spent five years in the Holy Land, from 1188 to 1193, immediately prior to and as part of the Third Crusade, from which he returned covered in glory. He had been appointed Lord of Jaffa and Caesarea by Richard Coeur de Lion and might well have become governor of Cyprus had he elected to remain, but it seems that he felt his real place was back home in Lusignan, possibly because he was the eldest surviving brother – the eldest, Hugh, having predeceased their father Hugh VIII of Lusignan and his younger brothers.

Here he ran into some trouble in 1203, when involved in a dispute with King John, King of England since 1199 on the death of Richard Coeur de Lion. In order to pursue some of their local claims the Lusignans, under Hugh IX, had besieged Eleanor of Aquitaine, King John's mother, in the castle of Mirabeau. The Lusignans were rather fond of this tactic in relation to Eleanor. They had after all ambushed her back in 1168 in an effort to win back Lusignan castle when it had fallen into the hands of her husband, Henry Plantagenet. More recently in 1199 they had waylaid her on the way to Spain to visit one of her daughters in order to extort the County of La Marche back from the Plantagenets. Now in 1203 there was trouble brewing on behalf of the 15-year-old Arthur, Duke of Brittany who had, it could be argued, prior claims to the English crown than John, as he was the son of one of his elder brothers. This claim was supported, not without self-interest, by the King of France.

All this had developed a more personal element for the Lusignans when, a few years previously, just as Hugh IX of Lusignan had been about to marry the beautiful Isabelle of Angoulême, John had whipped her away and married her himself – with which presumably she concurred, as becoming Queen of England was a considerable advance in her prospects. It obviously rankled however with the Lusignans.

The attempted seizure of Eleanor of Aquitaine at Mirabeau went disastrously wrong however, when John, not generally renowned for his military exploits, rescued her in a dawn raid that seems worthy of his father Henry II at his best. As a result the Lusignans and their allies were taken prisoner, humiliated by being paraded with a rope round the neck on the back of an ass, imprisoned in various castles, some in England, and held to ransom.

Geoffrey's ransom was subsequently paid by his young wife Humberge of Limoges, whom the old warrior had recently married, and who had given birth to the second Geoffrey in 1202. The unfortunate Arthur disappeared, presumed assassinated by King John, some reckoned strangled by his own hand before being dumped in the Seine. John had that kind of reputation.

The younger Geoffrey appears to have been quite a wild character, unpredictable and turbulent, perhaps inheriting the martial attributes of his father yet without having the opportunities to express them that had come the elder Geoffrey's way. He developed a fearsome reputation in view of his penchant for settling disputes by violence, not least a longstanding one with the abbey of Maillezais to which (according to both Geoffreys) some of their domain had been wrongfully attributed at its foundation. At one time the monks were driven from their abbey for several months and it was burnt down. As a consequence Geoffrey was roundly condemned and excommunicated, until in 1232 he was obliged to make a penitential trip to Rome and pay reparations to the abbey. Something of a comedown for one who is said to have had as a battle cry "There is no God!"

Less than ten years later he was in dispute with the King of France, the future saint, Louis XI, who after the Plantagenets had been expelled, gave much of Poitou to his young brother, Alphonse. This certainly upset the formidable Isabelle of Angoulême. After the death of King John in 1216 she had returned home and in 1220 married Hugh X of Lusignan. Somewhat bizarrely, this was the son of the Hugh IX she had jilted, but he had recently been killed crusading with King Louis in Egypt. (Even more bizarrely, the Hugh X she married had formerly been betrothed to Jeanne, her daughter by King John! Such were the convolutions of dynastic marriages.)

Isabelle then fomented a revolt against King Louis in which Geoffrey played a large part, if somewhat unsuccessfully. After being evicted from the castles of Mervent and Vouvant he had to take refuge in the forest, as the Lusignans had once been forced to do some seventy years before when defeated by Henry Plantagenet.

It appears, however, that Geoffrey was later reconciled to King Louis, for the castles of Mervent and Vouvant were restored to him. King Henry III of England (the son of Isabelle of Angoulême and the late King John) invaded in 1242. He was welcomed by Isabelle but defeated at the battle of Taillebourg. Whereupon he returned home, leaving Isabelle and Hugh X of Lusignan to throw themselves to the ground before the victorious King of France. From now on the Lusignans had to decide whom they regarded as their overlord, an absent King of England or a powerful and proximate King of France, and chose the latter. At any rate for the time being.

The eventful lives of the two Geoffreys stimulated the imagination of story tellers to write the romance of a single legendary figure, who was also incorporated into the romance of Melusine as one of her sons. A medal was even issued, showing his bust on one side, complete with boar's tooth, and a wild boar on the other.

Legend has it that two knights asked him to deliver their castle from a monster that had eaten an English knight. Geoffrey accepted the challenge but unfortunately fell ill and died before he could set out on the venture. The real life younger Geoffrey died in 1248 and was buried at the church of St Mary at Vouvant, where his body is said to lie to the left of the entrance.

Within a hundred years, however, the home branch of the Lusignan family died out. After Hugh XII in 1250 came Hugh XIII in 1270, Guy in 1302 and finally Yolande in 1308, who was declared non-hereditary and her lands confiscated by the King of France, Philip le Bel, in 1315.

From then on Lusignan became a property of the French crown until it passed into the hands of the Duke of Berry, brother of Charles V, on condition that he win it back from the English. He in turn, in pursuit of this task, as an early public relations exercise, commissioned the romance of Melusine.

Chapter Six

❧

The Faery Kin of Melusine

T HE faery kin of Melusine consist of her mother Pressine, and her sisters Melior and Palastine, who provide a fascinating backdrop to the main story. We also include the mysterious faery who was the first wife of Raimondin's father, Hervé de Leon, who raises another whole series of questions.

Pressine and the King of Albany

In part of Scotland that was also called Albany there once lived a brave king called Helinas, who had several children by his first wife, of which the eldest was a son, called Mataquas. Soon after the death of his wife he was hunting in the forest, close by the sea, when he was taken with a great thirst and rode towards a fountain that he knew to be there. As he approached, he heard singing so beautiful that he thought it must be from an angel.

He dismounted, tethered his horse to a tree, and made his way quietly toward the fountain, hiding in the bushes and branches. As he drew close to the spring he saw the most beautiful woman he had ever seen. He stopped, dazzled by her beauty, and crouched in the bushes, entranced by the sweetness of her song, forgetting all about the hunt and his thirst. So he remained until two of his hunting dogs ran up and began to leap round him joyfully.

Startled, like someone waking from a dream, he remembered the hunt, and his thirst, and without thinking, stepped out and went to the fountain. As he took up the basin that hung from a long chain and began to drink, his eyes fell on the lady, who had stopped her song. He greeted her respectfully.

"Madam," he said, "pray do not take it amiss if I ask who you are and of what family. For I know all the country round here and that there is no castle in these woods for at least four or five leagues. Hence my surprise to find someone as beautiful as you on your own. I trust I do not seem impertinent."

"Sir knight," said the lady, "I find no impertinence in you, but rather great delicacy and deference. I will not be alone for long. I sent my people ahead because I found this place so charming, and I was entertaining myself as no doubt you heard."

As she spoke a young squire arrived, elegantly dressed, leading a beautiful palfrey, richly harnessed.

The squire said to the lady: "Madame, it is time to come, if you please, for all is ready."

She thanked him, and then addressed the king. "Sir knight, I must now take my leave of you, but thank you for your company."

The king stepped forward and helped her to mount. She thanked him and departed, leaving him standing there bemused, so overcome by her beauty that he was no longer master of his acts. By the time his men came up he had lost all interest in the hunt.

"Go on ahead," he told them. "I will follow later."

They realised the king had something else on his mind and did as they were told, as he rode off in the direction taken by the lady.

He rode with such speed that he soon caught up with her, in a dense part of the forest. The lady heard the king's horse breaking through the branches in pursuit of her and said to her squire, "Stop and let us wait for the knight. I think he must have forgotten something at the fountain, or failed to tell us something he wanted to say, for he seemed very distracted."

The king rushed up to the lady as if he had never seen her and greeted her wildly, so smitten by love that he could hardly control himself.

The lady knew very well what was happening, but said to him, "King Helinas, why do you follow me in such haste? Have I taken something of yours?"

Helinas was amazed to hear her address him by name, and replied, "Dear lady, you have taken nothing. But as you have crossed my land I thought I had been most discourteous, as you are a stranger, not to have received you more worthily."

"If that is all it is," replied the lady, "I willingly excuse you. And if you want nothing more, that scruple need not detain you."

"My dear lady," the king burst forth, "I desire with all my heart something much more than that."

"And what is that? Don't be afraid to say."

"Dear lady, as you ask, I will tell you. I desire – before anything – your love!"

"Oh well," said the lady, "if that is all you wish, you can have it – as long as your intentions are honest, for I would never consent to be any man's mistress."

"Ah dear lady," cried the king, "I had no such low thoughts!"

"Then," said the lady, who knew perfectly well that he was inflamed with love for her, "if you wish, you can take me for your wife, as long as you swear that, if we have children, you do not attempt to see me during child bearing."

The king gave his promise (he would probably have agreed to anything!) and thought no more of it.

They were married, and lived happily together, even though the people of Scotland often wondered who this lady might be, with her great wisdom and ability for governing. But Mataquas, the king's son by his former marriage, hated her.

One day, being pregnant, her term arrived and she brought three daughters into the world. The eldest was called Melusine, the second Melior and the third Palastine.

King Helinas was not present but his son Mataquas went to find his father and said, "Madame the Queen has given birth to three prettiest little girls, you must come and see them."

Forgetting his promise to his wife, King Helinas went straightway and rushed into the room where Pressine was lying. At the sight of her and their three daughters, he cried "God bless you all!"

Pressine's response was terrible.

"Traitor, you have broken your promise! You have brought misfortune on yourself and lost me forever! I know very well that your son Mataquas brought this about, and I will be avenged on him and on his descendents, through my sister, the lady of the Lost Island!"

Then taking her three daughters with her, she vanished and was never seen in that country again.

When Helinas realised he had lost Pressine and his daughters, he was so distraught he knew not what to do. For eight years he did nothing but piteously lament. People said he had become mad, and gave the government of the country to Mataquas, who ruled well, treating his father with affection. The Scottish barons married the prince to an orphan, who was lady of Duras and Florimond and knew much distress in her life, but that is another story.

When Pressine left Helinas she went off with her three daughters to the Isle of Avalon, which is also called the Lost Island, because only chance will reveal the way to it, even for those who have been there before. There she brought up her daughters until they were fifteen years old. Every morning she took them to a high mountain called Eleneos, which translated means "the mountain of flowers", from whence the land of Scotland could be seen.

She told them, weeping: "My daughters, there is the country where you were born, and where you would have had your heritage, but for your father's betrayal. He has plunged us all into misery that will have no end until the Day of Judgement, when the Sovereign Judge will punish the wicked and reward the good."

Melusine asked, "What did our father do to bring about our sad fate?"

Pressine then told them her story.

Melusine asked more questions. What town and castle did they have in Albany? What were they called? Thus conversing, they descended the mountain and arrived back in Avalon.

Melusine then took her sisters Melior and Palastine on one side and said, "Dear sisters, see what misery our father has brought us and our mother, when we could have lived in earthly riches and honour. Can we do nothing about this? I think we should take revenge for all the trouble he has caused us. Should we not make him feel the same?"

The others replied, "You are the oldest, we will agree with whatever you say."

"Indeed, sisters," said Melusine, "you show a true filial love towards our mother. I have thought, if you agree, that we could shut him up in the magic mountain in Northumberland called Brumborenlion, from which he can never escape."

Her sisters replied, "Let's do it now! We really want to see our mother avenged of his treason."

The three sisters, using their faery powers, abducted Helinas and enclosed him in the mountain. Then they went to find their mother and told her what they had done.

"Mother, you need no longer grieve about the disloyalty of our father, for he now has his punishment. He can never leave the mountain of Brumborenlion and will pass the rest of his life there in misery!"

"Ah," cried Pressine, "perverse and evil daughters, with hard and bitter hearts. You have acted with deceitfulness and cruelty against he who gave you birth. From him I enjoyed all the pleasure I had in the world and now you have shut him away from me. Well, you too will be treated as you deserve!

"You, Melusine, are the eldest, and should have been the most sensible. It is because of you that your father suffers this painful imprisonment and you will be the first to be punished. The force of his paternal seed would have attracted you and your sisters toward his human nature. You would have only been a little time under the law of nymphs and fays, without ever returning to it.

"But from now on I strike you with the following curse. On every Saturday you will be a serpent from the navel downward. But if you can find a man willing to marry you who promises never to see you on a Saturday, (or if he should discover your condition, never to tell anyone), you can follow the course of earthly life of a normal human woman and die naturally like one. In any case, he will beget from you a noble and important line that will accomplish great things.

"But if your union is broken, know that you will return to the torment you were in before, for ever, until the day when the Sovereign Judge takes his seat. And you will appear each time when, three days later, the fortress that you have built and named after you changes hands, as well as each time one of your descendants is about to die."

"As for you Melior, I shall put you in a rich and powerful castle in Armenia where you will guard a hawk until the Day of Judgement. Any knight of noble blood may for three days and nights at midsummer attempt to watch over the hawk without sleeping. Should he fail to stay awake he will remain for ever a prisoner at the castle. But should he succeed you will appear before him on the fourth day, when he may receive from you any gift that he desires, as long as it is not your body or your love. Any who demand that gift will be forcefully expelled, lose prosperity, and their line be cursed unto the ninth generation.

"And you Palastine will be enclosed in a mountain guarded by a ferocious giant, perilous serpents and wild beasts, to watch over your father's treasure until the day when a knight – who must be of our lineage – comes to take the treasure, use it to conquer the Holy Land, and at the same time deliver you."

Overwhelmed with sorrow, the three sisters left their mother. Melusine went off to the great woods and groves of Poitou, Melior to the Castle of the Hawk in Greater Armenia, Palestine to mount Canigou in Aragon.

King Helinas lived a long time in the magic mountain until the day of his death, at which time Pressine arrived and laid him in a magnificent tomb in a chamber of incomparable riches and perpetual lamps that burned day and night. At the foot of the tomb she put a beautiful life size alabaster statue of herself which held a golden tablet on which was recorded the story of Helinas and Pressine. At the same time she installed as guardian of the place a line of ferocious and terrible giants who held the whole country in their power until the coming of Geoffroy Great-Tooth.

Comment

We find a number of minor inconsistencies in this story in the romance that has come down to us, which is not perhaps surprising as the romancers were not particularly knowledgeable about faery lore, and filled in with their own ideas what they did not know or understand. So it falls to us to try to sift some of the wheat from the chaff and to speculate on what of value may have been thrown away.

If we are to take their story at face value it casts a harsh light upon the faery world, where daughters take revenge on their father, and their mother punishes them savagely in turn. Whilst this is perhaps a needful corrective to sentimental portrayals of sugar plum fairies from a Victorian nursery world, we need to ask if it all really is or was as savage – indeed as inhuman – as this.

There has been a slow sea change in popular perception of faery over the centuries. In medieval times it was looked at with great suspicion through the eyes of the church, which tended to equate it with the demonic, even though more liberal elements allowed faery belief to continue in fairly sanitised ways such as portrayal as ancient local saints.

In the time of Shakespeare and Drayton they became miniaturised, although Oberon and Titania could still be pretty powerful, possessive and indeed spiteful, whilst Ariel and Puck played a more neutral role as servants to human magi or faery rulers, with the likes of Pinchblossom and Mustardseed perhaps laying the ground for later nursery sentimentality, although collections of folk tales by the Brothers Grimm and others showed a pretty harsh world. It was left until our own times and the vision of William Sharp, Yeats, Tolkien and others (not least R.J. Stewart), to bring about a further reassessment as to what this Otherworld might really contain.

Another point at issue is Pressine's status as a faery. If we are to accept the romancer's assumption that she is the sister of Morgan le Fay we find ourselves in the wide and complex realms of Arthurian legend. And within this, much hangs upon the nature of Morgan le Fay.

For it seems that in the deeper levels of Arthurian legend we are in a strange borderland *between* the human and the faery worlds. Morgan le Fay was the half sister of King Arthur, having been one of the daughters of his mother Ygrain by Gorlois, Duke of Cornwall. She would thus appear to be of human kind although in her life she hovers uncertainly between the human and the faery worlds. She is after all called Morgan *le Fay*, that is to say "the faery", and is capable of some startling feats of transformation, changing herself and her followers into a stone circle when hotly pursued.

Academic theory, insofar that it accepts a Celtic origin for Arthurian legend, tends to see the older characters as ancient gods, and dismisses Faery as a halfway stage on the way from god to human figure – from battlefield goddess like the Morrigu to flighty wayward woman like Arthur's half sister. They fail to give Faery any credit for being a level of reality in its own right – which is where they may make a great mistake.

Indeed, although the Arthuriad, particularly as it has come down to us via the bluff English rendering of Sir Thomas Malory, seems to take place entirely in the human world, there are strong grounds for regarding it as being much more closely involved with the world of Faery. In *The Faery Gates of Avalon* I have tried to show how early Arthurian romances depict a faery woman initiating a knight into the Otherworld.

As has been well documented by Laurence Harf-Lancner in *Les Fées aux Moyen Age* there are two types of tales of faery/human intercourse: one where the human is taken into the faery world (*les contes Morganien*), and the other where the faery enters the human world *(les contes Mélusinien)*. There are strong grounds for regarding even Queen Guenevere as a faery of the Melusinian type,* but that is another story!

The situation is further confused in the Melusine romance, where although Pressine may be an out and out faery, her marriage to the human King Helinas implies that her children Melusine, Melior and Palastine are only half faery. However, there is no mistaking in the main tale that Melusine and her sisters are very much of the faery kind, even though Melusine (as indeed Pressine before her) has been very successful in passing herself off as a flesh and blood human being.

Pressine's curse, with its savagery and bizarre detail, may have been fabricated by the romancers, or those who went before them, to account for events in Melusine's story – her serpent form on a Saturday and need to find a husband who would keep the matter secret so that she could live and die as a human woman. The implication is that the faery world is inferior to the human one, and in some respects almost like a place of purgatory.

Couldrette, as a clerk in holy orders, tries to show that Melusine's willingness to forgive Raimondin is a quality she lacked when she took revenge against her father. Thus suggesting a fundamental difference between faery and human worlds. Wondrous beauty but remorseless law with the faeries, much imperfection but a spirit of tolerance and forgiveness with the humans. He may have a point – along with a reason for a faery to seek experience of the human condition.

We have further ambivalence in the romancers' topological or geographical assumptions. Where exactly are, and what are the status of the magic mountains in question? The one, Eleneos, from which Pressine and her daughters can view the land of Albany, and the other, Brumborenlion, in which King Helinas is imprisoned. Are they in the physical world or the Otherworld? They seem to partake of both.

There is also "the Isle of Avalon, which is also called the Lost Island, because only chance will reveal the way to it, even for those who have been there before." Where Pressine and her daughters dwell seems pretty well an Otherworldly location, accessible from the human world but only under certain conditions.

* See *Red Tree, White Tree* by Wendy Berg (Skylight Press, 2010).

There are indeed places in the world where the veil is particularly thin, around which is built up a particular reputation. My personal preference would be to see Eleneos as the inner side of the Eildon Hills on the Scottish borders, and identify Brumborenlion with Bamborough Head on the northeast coast of England, that is sometimes associated with Sir Lancelot's castle of Joyous Garde. However, all are entitled to their own suppositions.

The accounts of Melusine's sisters show them to be guardians of treasures. Melusine too, in popular lore, guarded treasure deep under her castle, where she could be heard moving it about from time to time. Her sisters, however, also oversaw tests of those who sought their treasure – even as, in some respects, Melusine could be regarded as proving a test for Raimondin in the ability to keep faith and his word in return for the wealth and power he received from her. These elements of initiatory testing may well be a truer reason for faery impingement upon the human world than a consequence of their expiating family sins.

In each case however, in the romance, their function is tailored to fit the Lusignan story.

Melior at the Castle of the Hawk

There is a castle in Greater Armenia belonging to the faeries that bears the name of the Castle of the Hawk. Here if any noble knight could watch over a hawk, without sleeping, for the three days and nights preceding Midsummer Day, he could ask a gift from the lady of the castle. This could be whatever he desired, apart from possession of the lady herself – who was Melior, Melusine's sister and a daughter of the faery Pressine. Any who failed would remain forever a prisoner.

One year there came a king of Lesser Armenia, a fine knight, single, full of valour, who in all the ardour of youth, determined to watch in the Castle of the Hawk. He presented himself at the castle door, carrying a fowl with which he intended to feed the hawk, and was greeted by an man of great size, dressed all in white, who appeared to be very old. Learning that the king desired to submit to the custom of the place he led him up the steps to a great hall, furnished in great splendour, which contained the hawk on its perch, a beautiful and gracious bird.

The king said that he could easily watch without sleeping and would take good care to feed the hawk, and after these words was left there alone, absorbed in contemplation of the splendours that surrounded him.

He watched for a day and a night without sleeping, attentive and carefully feeding the hawk. Seeing around him wines and meats in abundance, and all sorts of provisions, he also ate his fill.

On the morrow he watched all day and then all night without a break and continued to feed the hawk. Beyond the bird he noticed an open door, and upon entering discovered yet more splendours. He had never seen such richness. The whole chamber was gilded with fine gold, and around the walls were portraits of knights, each with their coat of arms. Above the portraits were their names and on most of them the inscription: *In this year, this knight watched here, but could not stop from sleeping. He must live here to serve and honour us, without ever leaving, until the Day of Judgement.*

At three places, however, the portrait and coat of arms were surmounted with the inscription: *In this castle, in this year, a knight came who watched our hawk without sleeping as the test required. He left with the gift that he earned by his wisdom and diligence.*

The walls were also covered with paintings showing the lands and foreign places from whence the successful knights had come, along with the gifts they had carried away. The king dreamed so long of these splendours that he almost fell asleep but quickly left the chamber and successfully stayed awake.

On the morning of the fourth day the lady Melior duly appeared before him, dressed all in green. The king saluted her courteously and she said to him graciously: "You have bravely passed the test. Now tell me the gift of your choice. Ask whatever you wish."

"Great thanks, sweet and noble lady," replied the king, "but be assured that I want nothing other than you."

At these words she was incensed and said: "Poor fool, you know you cannot have that! Ask for something else!"

But he replied, "I want you, or nothing!"

The lady furiously replied, "Then since you are so obstinate, you will have nothing! You have lost the game. The only gift you will have is the misfortune that will follow you. You can never have me, either as mistress or as wife. And as you will not renounce your folly, bad luck will strike you and all your lineage, be sure of that! Those who succeed you and govern your realm will end by losing a war, the kingdom and their land. The last of them will carry the name of the king of the animals. All this will come to pass, believe me, every single word. Without your sinful thoughts, your folly and your overweening pride, you could have been blessed instead of cursed. Now leave this place, or risk more immediate punishment!"

The king now tried to seize her, but she vanished before his eyes. He felt himself seized and struck with blows from all sides and was thus driven from the place in shame and torment, bruised black and blue.

Although he had a long reign his fortune never ceased to decline, his country became depopulated, was desolated and ravaged, and many times he cursed the day when he had tried to possess the faery. When he left this world the king who succeeded him had a reign twice as bad, and so it continued until the ninth generation. Then the kings of Little Armenia lost their land and their goods and knew nothing but misfortune. The last of them was named Léon.

Comment

There is much faery lore in this traditional tale which appears to be grafted onto the story of Melusine to account for the fate of another branch of the Lusignan family.

It first appeared in the *Otia Imperialia* of about 1210 by Gervais of Tilbury, unconnected with Melusine and situated in Provence. It also featured in *Les Voyages de Mandeville,* a book of very tall stories and travellers' tales in 1350. Whether or not Jean d'Arras and Couldrette relied upon these sources we do not know.

In essence it represents a test of knightly and indeed magical virtue in being able to approach an Otherworld test and pass it successfully in all its ramifications. The fact that it takes place at the three days and nights leading up to Midsummer, along with reception at the door by a tall ancient man dressed in white, suggest its Otherworldly ambience.

It requires a commitment to belief in an Otherworld gateway at which one may present oneself and be amply rewarded if one successfully meets the conditions, fulfilling one's required duty of feeding the hawk, undiverted by the wonders of the place. It is, above all, a test of dedication, stamina and self control. However that is not quite all, for it also needs the ability to confront the power and beauty of a faery being without becoming glamourised. A test for those who undertake magic as a means of finding a sexual partner.

There is something of this impersonal element in the character of the hawk itself. As any manual of falconry will tell you, a hawk is not a bird that forms a loving relationship with its keeper. It conforms to the falconer's will because the falconer shares its aim, an accessory to its will, in the quest for prey. In short, it is not a pet – any more than a faery is likely to be.

This tale, attached to the story of Melusine, is a means of introducing another family dynamic, that of the Lusignans of Lesser Armenia, the last of whom was named Léon. Hence the punning reference to the last of the line of he who passed the test but tried to possess the tester being named after the king of the beasts.

King Léon V of Lesser Armenia was an historical character who was contemporary with the writing of the Melusine romance. After losing his kingdom to the Turks he was imprisoned for some time in Egypt and on his release came to the west to try to organise a crusade to restore his fortunes. He was singularly unsuccessful in this but was generously treated and sheltered by the King of France. He died in November 1393 and was buried at the convent of the Celestines in Paris. The funeral caused some wonder at the time for, according to the Armenian rites, the mourners wore white instead of black.

As King of Little Armenia he was said to be the last of the line that descended from the king who so spectacularly failed the test of Melior, predicted to suffer increasing misfortune and lose their lands over the space of nine generations. However the predictions, as is the general way of such things, came after the event.

Palastine at Mount Canigou

Palastine, the youngest sister of Melusine, was confined in Mount Canigou in the country of Aragon, guarded by a fearsome giant and many serpents and wild beasts. Here she watched over her father's treasure until some knight could win it as an aid to going on to win the Promised Land. However, Pressine had predicted that no one could perform that feat unless he were of her lineage.

Of the many knights who came to try none were ever seen again. Although Couldrette tells the story of one of them, an English knight, about 30 years old, gracious, learned and well skilled in the arts of war, who had been brought up since infancy at the court of King Arthur, and was of the lineage of Tristan, whom he calls the best knight in the world.

Having heard tell of the great treasure he declared he would go to Mount Canigou and endeavour to win it and then go off to conquer the Promised Land. He left for Aragon accompanied by a young page and on arrival asked to be shown the mountain. They warned him that the monster who lived there was of prodigious cruelty and ferocity, with a belly as big as a wagon. It was a fantastic beast of huge size, with no nose, only one ear, and with a single eye, three feet in circumference, in the middle of its forehead. It breathed through its ear and when it slept the whole mountain rang with the sound of its snoring. Its pit was right before the house of Palestine, and within this pit was an iron door that had never been opened. Behind this lay the treasure.

This was at the top of a steep slope, and many men had perished simply trying to climb it, for it contained a number of grottos and holes full of dangerous snakes and other terrible dangers. There was only a little narrow pathway that went upward for three leagues, with no place on either side in which to rest. And because of the serpents, of which there was an infinite number, no one who attempted to climb it had ever returned.

Nonetheless, the knight went off up the path, making the sign of the cross and consigning himself to God. First a mighty serpent, ten feet long, arose and advanced toward him, its great jaws open, intent on eating him there and then, but the valiant knight drew his sword and cut off its head with a single blow.

The knight continued his climb, and met with a great bear which attacked him at great speed. Without retreating a step the knight advanced on it with drawn sword. The bear gripped his shield and struck the knight's shoulder, tearing the coat of mail as the shield fell to the ground. The knight struck at the snout of the bear with his sword and cut away a foot of flesh. He did not fear being bitten now but it did not stop the bear from raising a paw to seize the knight. However he jumped lightly to one side and with a backward stroke cut off the paw. The bear, now furious, rose up on its hind legs and approaching the knight, caught him with its other paw, tearing through his armour. Both fell together, the knight trying to break away. He drew his dagger and forced it into the animal's throat. The bear left its hold, at which the knight cut off its other paw and then without respite, struck it in the body, forcing his sword up to the hilt. The bear gave a terrible cry and fell dead.

The good English knight continued his climb and ravaged all the serpents and beasts that he met. Finally he reached the top of the path that led to the monster's den. Here he met his match. As he jumped into the pit, the monster, enflamed with rage at the sight of him, advanced furiously. The knight drew his sword and struck a great blow with it, but to no effect, for nothing could wound the beast, neither iron, nor wood, nor steel. The monster simply took the sword in its teeth, broke it in two, and with gaping jaws, made just one mouthful of the knight and swallowed him whole.

That was his sad end. Never did any climb as high into the faery mountain as did this good English knight. His page waited two days at the foot of the mountain and then returned home to tell the story of his fate, learning the detail of all these terrible events through a divine who lived within that region, had studied in Toledo, and once been a disciple of Merlin.

Comment

Once again we find a source for this story in Gervais of Tilbury's *Otia Imperialia* and the marvellous legends attached to Canigou.

> "There is in Catalonia, in the bishopric of Gerona, a very high mountain, which the inhabitants call Canagum. Its perimeter is steep and for the most part inaccessible. At its summit is a lake with very black waters and bottomless; within which is to be found, they say, the habitation of demons, as vast as a palace, with closed doors, but the house and the demons remain unknown as they are invisible to ordinary people. If you throw a stone or some other heavy object into the lake, a storm will break out immediately, as if the demons were infuriated."

Gervais also tells the story of a father who, exhausted by the tears of his daughter, gave her to the demons. She spent seven years in Canigou before being rendered back to him "grown up, emaciated, dark skinned, horrible to see".

The role of Palastine is mentioned in the prose romance of Jean d'Arras but the story of the English knight appears only in the version of Couldrette, his patron at the time having a greater sympathy for the English than the French side in the Hundred Years War. There is not a great deal of mythopoeic interest in it, as the horrors encountered seem to derive more from a Christian idea of hellish monsters than from Celtic mythology.

Nonetheless the idea of a crusade was still being kept alive as late as the 15th century by those with a vested interest in it, and so Palastine plays her part in keeping this forlorn hope alive. It is perhaps of interest that only a Lusignan should be considered able or worthy to gain the treasure to enable reconquest of the Holy Land in view of their long historical record there.

There is a similarity between the story of the English knight at Canigou and that of Geoffrey Great-Tooth in Northumberland. And at the end of Geoffrey Great-Tooth's story he is invited to take on a task that has been failed by an English knight. But although willing to take it on Geoffrey is defeated by old age and dies before he is able to undertake the quest. Thus Palastine's treasure was never recovered and the Holy Land never recovered by the Crusaders.

The first wife of Raimondin's father, Hervé de Leon

Raimondin's father originally came from Brittany. His name was Hervé de Leon and he possessed great lands in Guérande, Penthiévre and all the surrounding region. He was an impetuous youth who feared nothing, was full of vivacity and daring, and because of this the King of Brittany held him in great affection and made him his seneschal.

But the king had a nephew, who at the instigation of certain envious people was persuaded that the king wanted to disinherit him and make Hervé his heir. So one morning, he armed himself and lay in wait for Hervé and leaped out upon him with drawn sword and dagger. Hervé wrested the sword from the youth's hand and struck him with the hilt to the side of the head. He meant only to stun the young man but alas found he had killed him.

Innocent or not, Hervé realised that a plot was closing round him, gathered together what money he could and fled. He travelled far into the high mountains which form the source of the Rhône and other great rivers that flow to the south. There he met a beautiful lady who, to his amazement, knew all that had occurred. He fell in love with her, they married, and she helped him to build many fortresses and towns. Soon this wild and desolate region became a prosperous and thriving county which, because it had been covered in forests when they came, they decided to call Forez. Which is still its name today.

Then some problem came between the lady and the knight which has never been disclosed. All we know is that she left him suddenly. Hervé was greatly afflicted but nonetheless his honour and prosperity continued to grow. The nobles of the country found him another wife of high birth, the sister of the Count of Poitiers, who gave him several male children, the third of whom was Raimondin.

The rest we know, for this was the Raimondin who subsequently married Melusine.

Comment

This story seems merely a duplication of the story of Melusine and Raimondin, although taking place beforehand and without a disastrous ending, although what happened to the faery bride and why she left Hervé is never mentioned.

Yet Melusine knew all about Hervé de Leon's history, for after her marriage she charged Raimondin to journey to Brittany to seek justice and restoration of Hervé's reputation and of his lands.

Intriguingly, she also said *"even if your father did kill the nephew of the king, he was in the right, and defending his life, but in light of what he had done he could not stay in Brittany and was exiled to the region that is known today as Forez. There, a lady, of whom I do not wish to speak, helped him greatly."*

How much, we may ask ourselves, did Melusine know of the identity of this companion of Raimondin's father whose story so much parallels her own? Indeed could it possibly even have been herself? Or was she one of a number of faery ladies who sought human husbands and experience at this time?

Chapter Seven

✧

ℳelusine ℭoday

NE thing that distinguishes Melusine in the annals of faery romance is her serpent tail. It has been the root of many comments from the academic (medieval folklore studies) to the irreverent (Rabelais likened it to a sausage!); from the anthropological (vestiges of Scythian serpent worship in the Roman legions) to the erotic (seen as a gigantic clitoris); from the religious (serpent in the Garden of Eden) to the fictional – which paradoxically, being of the imagination rather than the intellect, probably gets as close to truth as any!

Even more paradoxically, the most pertinent work of fiction does not deal with Melusine at all but with a close cousin of hers, the Vouivre – the serpent goddess who baulks large in the lore of the Jura mountains in southern France. She has been powerfully evoked in a novel called *La Vouivre* by the French writer Marcel Aymé. The title is untranslatable, but an English language edition published by the Bodley Head in 1949 chose to call it *The Fable and the Flesh*.

This title was cunningly chosen because it aptly sums up one of the problems we have in considering Melusine and her like. Where do we draw the line between imaginative fantasy and physical reality? For the two states impinge upon each other more radically than is often realised.

The vouivre is a surpassingly beautiful Otherworld woman who walks through the land accompanied by a concourse of snakes. Simply dressed, she wears on her head a diadem surmounted by a priceless ruby. She wanders the countryside of Franche-Comté, where she bathes in rivers or lakes, leaving her clothes on the bank along with her diadem. Should anyone attempt to steal the jewel they are attacked by serpents and done to death.

In Marcel Aymé's version of the story, a young peasant, Arsène Muselier, sees her bathing, but is more attracted to her as a woman than by the ruby. The vouivre, who has been walking the land for thousands of years, before there were even any humans to lust after her or covet her riches, is much touched by this. As a result she dallies for some time in the district before moving on, to make a closer study of how humans behave.

There follows a hilarious account of Arsène's problems in confessing to the village priest. For according to traditional religious teaching he has been having sexual intercourse with an infernal spirit. This is quite beyond the comprehension of the poor cleric, who is worried at what his bishop or the national press might say about the matter, should he appear to take Arsène's confession seriously. He would prefer not to believe in the vouivre at all.

The local mayor finds himself in a similar position, after a number of other people report sightings of the vouivre. This is something that, as a staunch rationalist republican, he just cannot accept. Both officials, of church and state respectively, would much prefer that the vouivre did not exist. Either she must be a figment of a simple peasant's imagination, or else some stray shameless foreign tourist.

This is much the situation we find in the modern attitude toward the world of faery. Granted that for the purpose of his novel Marcel Aymé has rendered the vouivre entirely physical, just as Melusine is held to be in her romance, as indeed are many of the mysterious damsels who lead knights on various quests in Arthurian legend. But should we not perhaps be seeking for a truth, a level of reality, that is halfway between "the fable" and "the flesh"?

By the very writing of this book, which is the culmination of many years of being led upon just such a quest, if you like, by Melusine, she has become something of a real presence in my own life. Just as she seems to have had a like effect upon Dr Matthew W. Morris, the American scholar who has devoted much of his life to translating both versions of her romance into English. Or indeed on various writers in France whose efforts we cite in our bibliographical notes.

A close friend of mine, in a state between sleeping and waking, recently heard a couple of times, quite clearly, a soft and warm woman's voice speaking very beautiful French. Two words seemed important but whilst my friend repeated them back to try to remember them, on waking they vanished. Frustrating! She later tried visualising the well described by R.J. Stewart in *The Well of*

Light and found herself diving into it and through an underwater arched door to come out in a pool she once used to visit. Back at the top of the well, as she looked down, the water began to stir, and a large snake with dragon-like head emerged. It turned into what appeared to be Melusine, who when asked what she wanted replied "Help to set me free!"

This seemed to mean "Make sure I am known of again". That is, to be present in human thoughts, perhaps respected, and loved!

Well, she seems well known enough in France, at any rate in Poitou and the southwest, but the retelling of her tale in the English speaking world would seem to be a good move toward wider recognition. Which is what this book is all about, in support of Dr Morris's more academic efforts.

In my own case it seems to have been a long haul, the culmination of following a number of seemingly irrational leads. It began back in 1959 when Margaret Lumley Brown, in an esoteric review, was struck by a powerful image of me in medieval times, in armour and in chains. Obviously a spot of bother at some point in the reincarnational record but not one that received any elucidation until 1973, when a psychic being consulted by a friend of mine on quite another matter drew attention to my being closely connected with a number of characters in the crusader kingdom of Jerusalem. Balian of Ibelin, Humphrey IV of Toron, and a number of others were mentioned. I tried a number of these on for size, so to speak, researching historical records but it was not until I realised that the one whom I could least conceptualise was the one who seemed closest to me, Amalric of Lusignan. He was certainly in such a pickle after the Battle of Hattin in 1187, and possibly a few years later, in 1193, after a bit of a run in with Henry II of Champagne.

This might well have remained as a bit of romantic fantasising that should not be taken too seriously – after all, it is how you deal with life in the present that really matters. But into life in the modern world came a strong and sustained impression to seek further. So much so that I spent eight years in part time study for an external degree in French at London University in order to get on closer terms not only with records of the crusader kingdoms but with the world of faery too.

This was not without odd occasions of "signs following" on the way. One was at a conference at the University of Wales at Lampeter on "The Grail, Arthurian Mysteries and the Grail

Quest" where I decided to devote my contribution of talk and short practical session to Melusine and the Lusignans. This included reference to Eleanor of Aquitaine and her rival in real life and in legend, Fair Rosamund. To some astonishment a photograph of both Eleanor and Rosamund appeared on the front page of the *Guardian* newspaper that morning! (13th August 1998.) It is not often that 12th century ladies find themselves featured so prominently in the modern press! Nothing to do with me of course, but one of those bizarre synchronicities that come an occultist's way.

Not only as a result of physical visits to Lusignan and Poitiers but from a deeper appreciation of the Arthurian romances of Chrétien de Troyes and Breton lais of Marie de France I began to get a feeling for the overseeing presence of Melusine. Which also led to the impulse, sustained over many months, to take the romances of Chrétien de Troyes and write them up for myself as if I were taking part in them, albeit as a looker on. From this experience came a realisation of the importance of faery in this early Arthurian work and my book *The Faery Gates of Avalon*.

And so in the course of time I began to become more and more consciously aware of the realm of faery, partly from a closer reading of Tolkien's faery work, and more so from R.J. Stewart's parallel endeavours. Not that I ever attended a workshop devoted to developing such contacts, rather they seemed more intent on contacting me.

They came sharply into focus with a sense of euphoria at a particular spot in a local park. Then I noticed that the ground round about was quite boggy, and realised I must be standing over a spring. And the focus for this was also a tree. I had never taken a great deal of notice of it before when walking the dog, but now I thought it would be interesting to identify it, and discovered it to be a rowan – the faery tree.

From then on, ever more conscious contacts seemed to be made with "the faery of the rowan tree" – to whom I dedicated *The Faery Gates of Avalon*. On one occasion I was urged to pluck a leaf, after which I had the quite palpable sensation of walking hand in hand with the faery round the park.

Now this is the kind of thing that one tends to keep to oneself, on the grounds that one might be thought, at best, a pathetic lonely fantasist, or at worst, on the verge of schizophrenia. However, to look on the positive side, it was not so far distant from the experience of Lanval, eponymous hero of a Breton lai of

Marie de France, who was told by a faery, "Whenever you wish to speak with me I shall be there with you, but no man but you will see me or hear my voice." I should say that in my case she only came when she felt like it. And on other occasions off her own bat when I was least expecting it. Which in a sense is reassuring, as it suggests that her existence was not entirely subjective on my part.

The contact was not physical (although the leaf may have played a physically talismanic part), but of the etheric and the imaginal. It would bring about an awareness of my own aura, which on the faery contact would seem to light up like a Christmas tree, along with an electric feeling of vitality, that could either be general, or focus on one or more of the etheric centres, particularly the solar plexus. The contact over time also brought about an intimate sense of awareness with trees and wildlife and growing things, and the stream, Pod's Brook, that ran at the foot of the hill. (I often wondered who Pod originally was, and whether of the human kind!)

Not that this contact seemed a direct one with Melusine. After my visit to Lusignan, she might come in at the level of the mind, with direct intuitions and ideas. Sometimes the urge to write a ritual, or less esoterically to draw pictures of her castle, either in the form that it might physically have taken, or in a more abstract magical form such as is described of one or two faery castles in Chrétien de Troyes – of a central tower with encircling wall containing four smaller towers at each of the cardinal points. To enter such a castle in vision could feel like entering into the conscious oversight of a great and friendly being. Or on other occasions I was encouraged to imagine adventures of characters within it, which I think was an endeavour to get me to think with less of the analytical mind (as is my wont) and more with the creative imagination. Or there was the physical impulse to buy the necessary paints and instruction book on calligraphy to depict her name in illuminated letters.

In short, these seemed to be simple acts of affection and regard as one might perform with or for a human friend, but for an inner guide. Above all, her precepts were in the direction of using the imagination. To have faith in the imagination. And in the importance of story, and above all of faery story.

Hence this book of the story of Melusine. Which might well be a lot truer than some people think!

Bibliographical Notes

HERE is little about Melusine published in English, apart from an article in Sabine Baring-Gould's *Curious Myths of the Middle Ages,* which suffers from some inaccuracies. Originally published by Longman in 1894, but reissued by Dover in 2005.

The version of the main story of the romance that I produce in Chapter 2 is in my own words, after reading with much enjoyment and instruction Matthew W. Morris's bilingual editions in Middle French and English and the edition of Jean d'Arras in Middle French by Louis Stouff (University of Dijon, 1932), and modern French translations of Jean d'Arras by Michele Perret (Stock, Paris, 1979 & 1991) and of Couldrette by Laurence Harf-Lancner (Flammarion, Paris, 1993). Also the anonymous 1500-20 English translation of Couldrette edited by Walter W. Skeat (Early English Text Society, Trubner, London, 1896). The two works by Matthew W. Morris are undoubtedly the ideal texts for an Anglophone reader, albeit, by their very nature, somewhat highly priced: *A Bilingual Edition of Jean d'Arras's Mélusine or L'Histoire de Lusignan,* and *A Bilingual Edition of Couldrette's Mélusine or Le Roman de Parthenay,* published by the Edward Mellon Press (Lewiston, Queenston & Lampeter, 2007 & 2003 respectively).

I have produced a collection of texts specifically on Melusine mostly translated from the French, entitled *The Book of Melusine of Lusignan in History, Legend and Romance* (Skylight Press, Cheltenham 2013). This includes Louis Stouff's almost definitive 1930 essay on the subject.

Two imaginative renderings of the Melusine romance by modern French writers are:
André Lebey, *Le Roman de la Mélusine,* Albin Michel, Paris 1925.
Claude Louis-Combet, *Le Roman de Mélusine,* Albin Michel, Paris 1986.

The first of these I have translated into English as *The Romance of the Faery Melusine* (Skylight Press, Cheltenham 2011).

A factually based novel but with a rationalistic bias on the origin of the faery is Marijo Chiché-Aubrun, *Les Dames de Lusignan* (Geste editions, La Creche, 2006).

Jean-Marie Williamson, *La fée et le chevalier,* is a part fictional account of the life of Geoffrey of Lusignan but quite tightly based on fact. (Éditions du deux rives, Nantes 2005).

Another novel worth reading that is mentioned in my text is Marcel Aymé, *La Vouivre* (Gallimard, Paris 1945) an excellent English translation of which was published as *The Fable and the Flesh* by Bodley Head, London 1949.

My own *The Faery Gates of Avalon* provides clues to faery tradition as found in the Arthurian romances of Chrétien de Troyes (Skylight Press, Cheltenham, 2013). As also do *Red Tree, White Tree* by Wendy Berg (Skylight Press, Cheltenham, 2010) and *Gwenevere and the Round Table,* also by Wendy Berg (Skylight Press, Cheltenham, 2012).

My book *Faery Loves and Faery Lais* (Skylight Press, Cheltenham, 2012) is my translation of a collection of Breton lais featuring faery material. *The Lais of Marie de France* are available in English (Penguin 1986) and provide a direct insight into 12th century Breton faery tradition. They are also available in the original French with glossary and student guide from Blackwell, Oxford, 1960. *La Fée et le chevalier* by Jean-Claude Aubailly (Champion, Paris 1986) gives a "mythanalyse" of them if from a somewhat psychological point of view.

In the more practical and esoteric sphere there is a considerable amount of sentimental and semi-erotic junk on offer but the works of R.J. Stewart can be highly recommended, perhaps *The Living World of Faery* (Gothic Image, Glastonbury, 1995) is the best to start on. There is more from him, much more, such as *Earth Light* and *Power Within the Land* (Element Books, Shaftesury, 1992) for the serious esoteric student, but see how you go.

There are two excellent scholarly books in French on the faery tradition in general:

Laurence Harf-Lancner, *Les Fées au Moyen Age* (Champion, Paris 1984) which is a comprehensive treatment dividing faeries into Morgan and Melusine types – the first attracting lovers into Faeryland, the second coming from Faeryland to join a lover on Earth.

Slightly less of an academic heavyweight, but not necessarily the worse for that is Pierre Gallais, *La Fée á la Fontaine et á l'arbre* (Rodopi, Amsterdam and Atlanta GA, 1992)

More specific books on Melusine include:

Jean Markale, *Mélusine* (Albin Michel, Paris 1993), a well known scholar of Celtic lore, if thought a little idiosyncratic in some quarters, but he knows his stuff, even if I do not go all the way with him on some of his psychological theories.

Françoise Clier-Colombani, *La Fée Mélusine au Moyen Age* (Le Leopard d'or, Paris 1991) which concentrates on the images of Melusine, with a comprehensive illustrated section of wood block reproductions and photographs.

Claude Lecouteux, *Mélusine et le Chevalier au Cygne* (Payot, Paris 1982) is useful for also covering the Knight of the Swan legends, otherwise available for English readers in the somewhat dated Robert Jaffray, *The Two Knights of the Swan* (Putnam, New York & London, 1910).

Also of interest is Boria Sax, *The Serpent and the Swan*, a study of the animal bride in folklore and literature (McDonald & Woodward, Blacksburg VA, 1998).

Sur les chemins de Mélusine by Michel Cordeboeuf (Geste, La Creche, 1999) is a sumptuously illustrated tourist book on sites associated with Melusine.

Somewhat more peripheral is *Melusine the Serpent Goddess in A. S. Byatt's "Possession" and in Mythology* by Gillian M. E. Alban (Lexington Books, Lanham 2003) an academic work which is not quite so specialist as its title may sound, for it covers much related mythology – apart from A S Byatt's famous novel, which is in any case well worth a read.